By Lori Wilde

All Out of Love
Love at First Sight
A Cowboy for Christmas
The Cowboy and the Princess
The Cowboy Takes a Bride
The Welcome Home Garden Club
The First Love Cookie Club
The True Love Quilting Club
The Sweethearts' Knitting Club

Available from Avon Impulse
One True Love

THE CHRISTMAS COOKIE CHRONICLES
Carrie
Raylene
Christine

One True Love

A Cupid, Texas Novella

LORI WILDE

This is a work of fiction. Names, characters, places, and incidents are products of the author's imagination or are used fictitiously and are not to be construed as real. Any resemblance to actual events, locales, organizations, or persons, living or dead, is entirely coincidental.

EPub Edition JUNE 2013 ISBN: 9780062219312

Print Edition ISBN: 978-0-06-221932-9

10 9 8 7 6 5 4 3

To the memory of my grandmother, Glenna Osborn Reid. I drew on the stories of her girlhood growing up in Texas in the 1920s while writing One True Love.

Chapter One

Whistle Stop, Texas. May 1924

I MET JOHN FANT on the worst day of my life.

There he was, the most handsome man I'd ever seen, standing at the bottom of my daddy's porch clutching a straw Panama hat in his hand, the mournful expression on his face belying the jauntiness of his double-breasted lightweight jacket and Oxford bags with sharp, smart creases running smoothly down the front of the legs. An intense, magnetic energy radiated from him, rolled toward me like heat waves off the Chihuahuan Desert. I felt an inexplicable tug in the square center of my belly.

His gaze settled heavily on my face. There were shadows under his eyes as if he'd been up all night, and there was a tightness to his lips that troubled me. A snazzy red Nash roadster sat on a patch of dirt just off the one-lane wagon road that ran in front of the house. It looked just as out of place as the magnificent man in my front yard.

My knees turned as watery as the mustang grape jelly I canned last summer that hadn't set up right, and suddenly, I couldn't catch my breath. I hung on to the screen door that I was half hiding behind.

"Is this Corliss Greenwood's residence?" he asked.

"Yessir." I raised my chin, and stepped out onto the porch. The screen door wavered behind me, the snap stretched out of the spring from too many years of too many kids bamming it closed. Without looking around, I kicked the door shut with my bare heel.

He came up on the porch, the termite-weakened steps sagging and creaking underneath his weight.

Shame burned my cheeks. *Please, God, don't let him put one of those two-tone wing tips right through a rotten board.*

He was tall with broad shoulders, and even though he was whip-lean, he looked as strong as a prizewinning Longhorn bull. A spot of freshly dried blood stained his right cheek where he must've cut himself shaving. He'd shaved in the middle of the day, in the middle of the week? His hair was the color of coal and he wore it slicked back off his forehead. His teeth were straight and white as piano keys, and I imagined that when he smiled, it went all the way up to his chocolate brown eyes, but he wasn't smiling now.

Mr. Fant had caught me indisposed. I must look frightful in the frayed gray dress I wore when cleaning. The material was way too tight around my chest because my breasts had blossomed along with the spring flowers. Strands of unruly hair were popping out of my sloppy braid and falling around my face. I pushed them back.

Another step closer and he was only an arm's length away.

My heart started thudding. His masculine fragrance wafted over to me in the heat of the noonday sun, notes of leather, oranges, rosemary, cedar, clove, and moss. Perfume! He was wearing perfume. I'd never met a man who wore perfume before, but it smelled mighty good, fresh and clean and rich.

My daddy always said I would have made a keen bloodhound with the nose I had on me. A well-developed sense of smell can be good for some things, like telling when a loaf of warm yeast bread is ready to come out of the oven, and inhaling a snout full of sunshine while unpinning clothes from the line, but other times having a good sniffer could be downright unpleasant—for instance when visiting the outhouse in August.

"Is Corliss your father?"

My throat had squeezed up, so I just nodded.

"I'm John Fant."

I knew who he was of course. The Fants were the wealthiest family in Jeff Davis County. Truth be told, they were the wealthiest family between the Pecos River and the New Mexico border. The Fants had founded the town of Cupid, which lay twenty-five miles due north in the foothills of the Fort Davis Mountains, and they owned the Fant Silver Mine where my father worked. Three years ago, when John had returned home with a degree from Maryland State College, his father, Silas Fant, had turned the family business over to his only son.

The screen door drifted open against my calf and I bumped it closed again.

He arched a dark eyebrow. "And you are . . . ?"

"Millie Greenwood," I managed to push my name over my lips.

"How old are you, Millie?"

The way he said my name sent a shiver shaking down my spine for no good reason. It seemed a nosy question and I was within my rights to go back inside and shut the door in his face. It wasn't proper for a young lady to have a prolonged conversation with a good-looking bachelor on her front porch without a chaperone present, but I answered him anyway. "I turned eighteen last week."

He flicked a glance over my shoulder. "Is your mother home?"

I'd sent my brothers and sisters off blackberry picking so I could clean the house after Mama took a BC powder and went to bed to sleep off one of her migraines, but I didn't want him to know I was basically alone. "She's inside."

"May I come in?"

"I'm not allowed to invite strangers into the house."

"I'm not a stranger, I'm your father's boss."

That was true enough. I hesitated, uncertain of what to do next.

"I'm afraid I've got some very bad news," he said in a soft voice. The expression in his eyes was far too kind.

"This isn't the sort of thing that should be discussed on the porch."

I went sick all over when he said that. This time, when the screen door hit me in the behind, I didn't close it, but instead held it wide open. "C'mon in."

A fly came in with us, buzzed lazy circles around the sitting room. My chest was so tight that I was having trouble breathing and my head pounded hard. Was I going to have to take a BC powder myself?

I waved at the sofa. "Please have a seat, Mr. Fant, while I fetch my mother."

He didn't sit, just stood there, holding his hat.

I slipped down the short hall to the bedroom my mother and father shared and knocked lightly on the door. "Mama, I called. "Mr. John Fant is in our sitting room."

Less than a minute later, the door wrenched open. My mother wore only a thin chemise and her hair was all mashed up on the side. Her face was ghostly pale, the way it got every time she had a migraine, but what scared me to death was the look of pure terror in her eyes. "John Fant is here? In our house?"

Mutely, I nodded.

The blue vein at the hollow of her throat pulsed fast. She ran her fingers through her hair and moved into the hallway.

I rested a hand on her shoulder. Her skin felt so cold. "Mama, you need to put on a dressing gown."

"Yes, yes," she murmured, disappeared into the bedroom only to poke her head out again. "What was I looking for?"

"Dressing gown."

The lump in my throat grew bigger with each passing second, and I struggled to keep my mind from leaping to conclusions, but dread settled into my bone marrow. I clenched my hands into fists, closed my eyes. *Please, God.*

Finally, Mama came back out, trying to cinch the belt of her faded pink floral dressing gown, but her hands were shaking so hard she couldn't manage it.

"Here," I said, and tied it for her.

"Thank you, Millie," she whispered, and cupped my cheek with her palm.

I took her hand and led her to the sitting room. Mr. Fant was still standing, still held that silly Panama hat that he was turning around and around in his hands.

He nodded at my mother, his face somber. "Mrs. Greenwood."

Mama drew a shuddering breath so deep that I felt it in my own body. "Mr. Fant."

"Please, sit down," he invited like it was his house instead of ours.

Mama sagged against me and made a soft mewling noise like a newborn kitten. I guided her over to the threadbare sofa. She wilted onto it and I perched beside her, making sure to sit on the grape jelly spot, permanently embedded into the fabric, so Mr. Fant couldn't see the stain.

He pulled up a Hitchcock chair from the corner of the room and sat down in front of us.

Mama was plucking restlessly at the lapel of her dressing gown, like she was picking off lint. I touched her hand so she would stop.

Mr. Fant's grim eyes met mine.

I curled my fingers into crabapple knots against my thighs.

He leaned over and laid his big palm on my closed fist. I was surprised to discover it was calloused like a workman's. I expected a man of Mr. Fant's status to have palms as smooth as a baby's backside. If the situation hadn't been what it was, I would have been both alarmed and excited by the feelings that his touch stirred, but considering the circumstances, I was just plain numb.

"Mrs. Greenwood, Miss Greenwood." He stopped, cleared his throat. "I'm afraid I have some tragic news."

"Just say it!" I blurted, unable to stand the tension one second longer.

"There's been a cave-in at the silver mine," he said gently. "I'm so—"

"No!" my mother wailed before he finished speaking, clutched her head in both hands, and began rocking to and fro. "No, no, no!"

I felt my mind break away from my body and drift up toward the ceiling. I was outside myself, watching the whole proceedings from afar. You could have slapped a scalding hot branding iron against my bare foot and I wouldn't have felt a thing.

"I deeply regret to inform you," he went on stoically, but the pain in his dark eyes gave him away. This event had touched him profoundly. "That Mr. Corliss Greenwood has lost his life."

We buried my father three days later.

John Fant paid for the funeral and those of the three other men killed in the cave-in. The entire Fant family came to the services, except for the children of course. I thought it was real nice of them to drive the twenty-five miles.

Mama was inconsolable. She'd been crying for three days straight and she could barely stand on her feet in the heat, even though the funeral director had erected a canopy over the gravesite. She leaned heavily against me throughout the preaching, handkerchief pressed to her face.

The preacher announced that we were ready to receive condolences from those paying their respects. I arranged my three brothers and three sisters in a stair-step row starting with the youngest, Daisy, who was four and kept asking when Daddy was coming home. I straightened the navy blue bows in her braids and wiped my six-year-old brother Pete's nose with the back of my sleeve. I wet my palm with spit and slicked down Jimmy's cowlick, gave Jenny a stern look because she was wriggling, smiled at Lila who was so shy she couldn't look strangers in the eye, and clamped Willie on the shoulder. Willie was next in age to me, sixteen, and now he was the man of the family. Then I went to the end of the line to keep Mama propped up.

The senior Mr. Fant leaned heavily on an ivory cane that contrasted sharply with his black suit and black bowler hat, and he solemnly shook the hand of every single Greenwood child, even Daisy, who looked confused by the whole thing.

Mrs. Fant's mouth was pulled tight and her eyes were so sad, as if it was *her* daddy who'd died. She wore black gloves like a real lady and her handshake was light as a hummingbird's wing. She skipped the younger kids, only stopped by Willie and me. I had a feeling that shaking so many hands would have been too much for her.

Penelope Fant Bossier came next. She was older than John by a year or two and she moved with such grace I felt like a dirt clod next to her. Rumor had it that she'd gone to a fancy finishing school back East and you could see it on her.

Her husband trailed behind her. Beau Bossier was barely taller than his wife, and stocky. He had thick wrists, a square jaw, and looked like he'd be good at hunting. He kept alternately tugging at his tie and mopping his ruddy face with a silk handkerchief.

And then there was John.

I gazed into his eyes and my heart skipped a beat.

"Millie," he murmured, his warm voice full of sympathy, and his big, strong hand enveloped mine. "I'm so sorry for your loss."

"Thank you, John," I said, shocking myself by using his first name.

My siblings gasped and stared at me openmouthed as if I'd tooted in church.

I don't know why I said it, except he'd been in our house and sat with us while he delivered the worst news you could give someone. And he'd just called me Millie, not Miss Greenwood. I guess it gave me a false sense of intimacy. A working-class girl like me didn't address an upper-crust man by his first name without being invited to do so, and even then, such familiarity was still frowned upon. Better to beg his forgiveness for taking liberties and calling him by his given name.

But then John smiled.

Apparently, he hadn't minded, so I didn't apologize, which was quite bold of me in front of everyone. On a day like today, breaking the rules of decorum could be forgiven without having to say you were sorry.

He dropped my hand and turned to my mother. "Mrs. Greenwood, there is no way to ease the suffering for what you have lost, but your husband was killed while in my employ and you are entitled to be compensated for the loss of income."

"What?" Mama whispered.

She hadn't been thinking beyond her own grief, but I'd already started worrying how we were going to make ends meet without Daddy's paycheck. We had a garden, a flock of chickens, two hogs, and a cow, but it required seed and feed to keep a farm going.

John withdrew a folded piece of paper from the pocket of his lapel and passed it to my mother.

I leaned over her shoulder as she opened it. She gasped, spread her fingers over her throat.

It was a check for five thousand dollars. More money than Daddy would have made in ten years.

Mama clutched the check to her chest. "Thank you, oh thank you. That's such a huge weight off my shoulders."

John shifted, glanced over at me, his eyes carefully hooded.

I couldn't read what he was thinking.

"It seems like a lot of money right now, Mrs. Greenwood," he said. "But you've got seven children to provide for."

Mama nodded.

"As further assistance to your family," Penelope spoke up then, "I'd like to offer your eldest daughter a job in service as a maid to my family."

A job? Me? Working for the richest family in the Trans-Pecos region? My pulse galloped.

"Millie?" Mama grabbed my arm with both hands, crushing the check against my skin. "You want to take my Millie away? She's my right hand."

"We would pay her forty dollars a month. She could send most of that home to you since she would be living in maid's quarters and we'd provide her food," Penelope explained.

My jaw unhinged. It was an absurd amount of money. Almost as much as my father had made working in the silver mine.

"I just can't bear the thought of not seeing her every day," Mama fretted.

"Cupid is just twenty-five miles away," John said. "We could have the chauffeur drive Millie home to visit you one Saturday a month and come back for her on Sunday evening."

Me? Riding in a chauffeur-driven car? I almost swooned.

"Oh my. You are so generous," Mama murmured.

"We owe you a great deal," John said solemnly.

Mama loosened her grip on me. "It's up to Millie."

"I don't have any experience as a maid," I mumbled.

"Everyone has to start somewhere," Penelope said brightly. "I saw how well you handled your brothers and sisters. You have more skills than you realize."

"Thank you, ma'am."

"Would you like the job?" Penelope prodded.

I loved my mama and my brothers and sisters with all my heart, but this was a chance for me to get out and see something of the world. Spread my wings. Start my own life.

"Yessmum." I curtsied because it seemed the thing to do.

"No need for that," Penelope said. "You'll soon find out we're like everyone else. Dirty socks on the floor, dust bunnies under the bed, water spots on the dishes. You'll work and work hard."

I pulled myself up straight and tall. "I'm not afraid of hard work."

"Excellent," Penelope said. "Then we'll expect you after a proper bereavement period. Perhaps a month?"

"I'd rather start right away," I surprised myself by saying. "I don't do well when I'm not busy."

"All right then. We'll send our chauffeur, Charles, to collect you tomorrow."

And just like that, I had a job.

Chapter Two

It turned out that the Bossier home was right next door to the Fant mansion. Silas and Margaret Fant had purchased the house as a wedding present for Penelope and Beau in 1916 after the previous owner was killed in the trenches during WWI. I learned that John too had served in the later days of the war, having turned eighteen that same year. That surprised me. I figured as the son of the elite, he would have received a deferment.

"Johnny wanted to serve," the Bossiers' cook, Mabel, said proudly when I posed that question.

It was odd, thinking of John Fant as a child called Johnny. He seemed far too worldly and masculine to have ever been anything but full-grown John.

Mabel had been with the Fants for fifteen years before she'd crossed the fence to work for Penelope. "I raised that boy as if he were my own. Gave him his first bite of oatmeal. Baked every single one of his birthday cakes until he went off to war and then on to college."

Her hair was the color of slate and she wore it twisted in a tight bun at the crown of her head. She been married once, but hadn't liked it much, and when her husband had run off with another woman, she'd decided that was that. But she flirted with the widowed butcher, because when she did, he gave her an extra ounce of meat, and that made Miss Penelope marvel at how well she stayed within the kitchen budget.

Mabel smelled of the apple cider vinegar that she sipped like a toddy. "Good for the digestion," she declared, and every time she ate something sweet—which was often three or four times a day—she'd swat her big, fleshy fanny, and flash a toothy grin. "Goes right to my hips, but that just means there's more of me to love."

And that made me wonder if she was telling the truth about just flirting with the butcher.

There were three of us who lived in the servants' quarters behind the manor—Mabel, me, and the gardener, an elderly man named Jorgie, who Mabel swore couldn't speak a lick of English, but had a thumb greener than God. After she said that, she slapped a palm over her mouth as if she thought she might be struck by lightning for saying it.

Jorgie's skin was brown and rough as dried shoe leather and he sang lively Mexican songs while he worked. The chauffeur, Charles Billsby, worked for the Fants. Charles quartered at the Fants' home, but he drove for Penelope and the children just as often as he did for Silas and Margaret, because none of them had ever learned to drive. Beau owned a Graham Brothers stake truck that he used to go back and forth from his gun store in Alpine.

John, of course, drove himself in that dashing Nash roadster.

"What happened to the last maid?" I dared to ask Mabel one day after the first week. I was washing dishes while she prepped the evening meal.

Mabel glanced over her shoulder like someone could be lurking inside the icebox behind her and lowered her voice. "Ruthie got herself into trouble."

"What do you mean?" I asked, images of gangsters, bootleggers, and gun molls hopping into my head. I had access to daily newspapers and penny dreadfuls in Cupid, and my imagination had gotten the better of me.

"You know. In the family way." Mabel pantomimed having a swollen belly.

"Oh," I said, slightly disappointed that Ruthie's departure hadn't been caused by something more lurid.

Mabel put up her hand to shield her mouth and whispered loudly, "It was the McClearys' oldest boy, Marcus."

"What was?"

Mabel looked at me like I was the densest turnip ever to fall off the truck. "That got her in the family way."

I nodded. I was a country girl. I knew where babies came from and how they got there.

"'Course he couldn't marry her," Mabel went on. "His family being who they were and her nothing but a maid."

"Who *are* the McClearys?"

Mabel clucked her tongue over my ignorance as she

had many times during the last several days. "Just the second richest family in Cupid."

"Oh."

"Marcus loved Ruthie to pieces, but the McClearys sent her off to have the baby in San Antonio at a home for unwed mothers and sent him off to college in California. Swept their little problem right under the rug. Miss Penelope was terribly embarrassed over the whole thing. She avoided the Ladies' League for weeks and she's the president."

"Why was she embarrassed? It wasn't her fault."

"Because she'd allowed that tomfoolery to go on underneath her nose." Mabel punched the bread rising in the big metal mixing bowl with a sharp, quick jab. "I could have told her. They were bumping and thumping the walls of Ruthie's room for hours on end—that boy had stamina—but I'm no snitch."

"I'm sure." I paused to dry my hands on my apron.

She shook a plump finger under my nose. "Learn a lesson from that, missy. We're the help. Steer clear of the gentry. 'Less you want to have the same fate as Miss Ruthie."

But of course, I knew that. Knew the rules of the social classes. Never cross that line or your life was ruined.

Still, I have to admit that I'd taken to gazing out the windows any time I was cleaning a room on the side of the house that bordered the Fant property, hoping for a glimpse of John coming or going. He still lived at home, with the understanding that the house would one day be his and that's where he'd live with his wife and children.

Tradition, I quickly learned, was a big deal to the well-heeled.

Penelope and Beau had two children that they sometimes asked me to watch after. I didn't mind that at all. I was used to kids and it kept me from missing my brothers and sisters too much.

Miss Adeleine, everyone called her Addie, was five years old and had auburn hair like her mother. She was bright as a copper button, and my first week there she came to me crying because her front tooth was wiggly, but she was too scared to tell her mother because Addie had been chewing on one of Mabel's cinnamon sticks and she thought that had caused it.

I was honored she came to me. I explained that everyone loses his or her baby teeth and told her a story about the Tooth Fairy, while I quietly slipped my hanky from my pocket, reached up, and plucked that loose tooth out of her mouth before she even knew what I was doing. After that we were fast friends, although Miss Penelope cried because she hadn't been the one to pull her first-born's first tooth, and that made me feel bad.

Ernest was three and still hanging on to his baby fat. He had a chubby round face and smiled all the time, but he did have a stubborn streak, and once that boy balked, there was no persuading him. You just had to pick him up, tuck him under your arm, and take him where you wanted him to go, all the while getting kicked in the side from his pudgy little legs still trying to run away. He was easy to figure out, though, and I learned how to head off the stubborn streaks before they started. Bribery worked like a charm. Give that boy a cookie and he'd do anything.

For the next three weeks, I stayed busy, which was good. Didn't leave much time for grieving over my daddy. Sometimes though, I'd catch a scent of his pipe tobacco and the loss would go all over me, grabbing my throat and wringing me up in knots. I thought the smell of tobacco was all in my imagination until one day when I was hanging out clothes, the scent drifted over to me on the breeze along with the fragrance of the honeysuckle that grew on the fence row between the two houses. I started feeling pretty melancholy.

Then someone coughed.

I peeked around the sheet billowing in the breeze and spied John Fant leaning against the side of the house, holding a pipe in one hand and shaking out a match with the other.

My daddy had smoked a corncob pipe, but John's looked real fancy. It had a black stem and a fat, glossy brown bowl that matched his two-tone wing tips. He had a worried expression on his face. I wondered what he had to worry about. He had all the money in the world. I didn't think he'd seen me watching him, so I went back to pinning clothes.

"Bad habit, I know," he called out. "I'm trying to give it up."

I leaned my head back so I could see him from around Miss Addie's pinafore. He wore only a dress shirt and a vest, no jacket, and he wasn't wearing a hat either. "I don't mind so much. My daddy smoked a pipe."

Bringing up my father killed the conversation and I went back to hanging up clothes, my muscles tense all over.

"Millie," he called again after a long moment.

"Yessir?"

"Could you come here a minute?"

My heart flew up into my throat. "Here?"

"To the fence where I can see you eye to eye."

Why did he want to look into my eyes? I gulped, stuck a clothespin on a kitchen towel, and then smoothed my hands against my apron.

I was scared to walk over there. Afraid someone would see us talking and it would spark gossip. Afraid that if John looked into my eyes he'd see what I was feeling for him. But I'd learned a long time ago it was better to face things head-on than run from them, so I eased over to the fence.

"Yessir, Mr. Fant."

"Call me John." He smiled. "Just like you did at the funeral."

So he remembered that. I felt my cheeks heat and ducked my head. "I can't call you John," I said. "It wouldn't be fittin'."

"Not in front of people, but when it's just you and me."

He said it like there were going to be more times when it would just be him and me. My knees went shaky. I wasn't going to end up like Ruthie, no sirree. "I think I'll stick with Mr. Fant."

"You're probably right." He took a long puff off his pipe.

I sneaked a glance at his face.

His gaze hit mine like bacon on a hot cast-iron skillet, and suddenly, I couldn't catch my breath. The urge to turn and run was so strong I could taste it on the back of my tongue, all dry and salty bitter like baking soda.

"I need your opinion on something."

"Mine?" I couldn't believe he was asking for my advice. "Why would you need my opinion?"

"It's about the silver mine."

Some of the breath I'd been holding leaked out of my lungs. I don't know what I thought I'd expected him to say, but this wasn't it.

He canted his head, his eyes still hanging on to mine. I wanted to look away, but just couldn't. "After the cave-in, after what happened to your father and those other miners, I'm thinking about closing the mine."

I ran a finger over the white picket fence, loaded with honeysuckle vines, that separated him from me, my fingers moving up and down with the spikes of each wooden picket, the mingling smell of pipe tobacco and sweet honeysuckle wrapping around us. "If you closed the mine, how would your family make money?"

A lazy smile lifted up the corner of his lips. "My family's got their fingers in a lot of pies."

"Sounds messy."

He laughed, and the sound pleased me all the way to the tips of my toes. "It certainly can be. Besides the silver mine, we've run cattle out west of town, have a couple of oil wells pumping on a patch of land we own in Pecos County, and we own half interest in a shipping company in Maryland."

"That sounds like a lot to keep up with."

"Multiple streams of income. Diversity."

I couldn't wrap my head around that, so I just nodded. I guess once you were rich, it wasn't all that hard to buy into other businesses and get richer.

"Actually, it's been costing us money to keep the silver mine open. After sixty years of mining, the ore is playing out."

My daddy had said the same thing about the silver mine. He'd worried about losing his job. "What about all those miners that will be out of work? What about those families that will go hungry?"

"That's why I'm asking your opinion. The mine is old and I'm afraid we'll have more cave-ins. We could bring in a crew, shore up the mine, but that will cost a lot of money. Money we probably won't recoup."

"So it comes down to dollars and cents."

"No," he said. "That's the dilemma. I know your community depends on the mine. Without it . . ." He shook his head.

Without it, there would be nothing to sustain my tiny hometown.

"The Christian thing to do would be to keep the mine open," I said.

His eyes searched my face. "Even if keeping it open means more men get hurt or killed?"

I blew out my breath. "My daddy knew what the job entailed when he took it."

He pushed a hand through his dark hair. "I can't in good conscience keep it open without restoring the mine."

"I'm sorry, Mr. Fant. I can't tell you what to do."

"Can you answer me one question?"

I notched my chin up. "I'll try."

"Given the facts of the situation, what would *you* do if you were in my shoes?"

"I'd make sure no one else's daddy had to die."

FOLLOWING THAT STRANGE conversation with John, I had a dream.

In the dream, my daddy was alive and looking like he always did. His thick, straight black hair parted straight down the middle so that it fell evenly on both sides. He had some Comanche blood in him, although he didn't like people to know since it wasn't that long ago that Comanches raised hell all through the Trans-Pecos region, but you could see his heritage in his high cheekbones and slightly flat features. He walked with that bowlegged gait that I'd recognize anywhere, and he was whistling his favorite song, Irving Berlin's "I Gotta Go Back to Texas."

He was dressed as usual in his silver-dusted work clothes and lace-up boots, and was wearing the worn-out straw cowboy hat that he kept hung on the hook beside the front door at home. The strangest thing was, he was wearing silver bells strapped to his boots and we were standing in the Fants' backyard.

Joy flooded me and my whole body was atremble. He wasn't dead! It had all been a big misunderstanding.

"Daddy," I said, thinking at the time that this wasn't a dream. "What are you doing here?"

He winked at me. "I always told you, sissy-babe, I'd dance at your wedding with bells on."

"But I'm not getting married!" I exclaimed, and then I glanced down and saw I was wearing a beautiful white lace wedding gown, like the kind you see in high-fashion magazines, with a long train that my sisters Jenny and Lila were holding fanned out behind me, and I had a bouquet of beautiful red roses with sprigs of white baby's breath clutched in my hand.

"Tell *him* that," Daddy said.

"What?"

Daddy nodded to someone behind me.

I turned around and there stood John at the top of the steps. He wore a black tuxedo with a single red rosebud tucked in the lapel. His eyes were full of love for me.

My heart started beating crazy fast.

"John?" I whispered.

"I'm here to give you away, sissy-babe," Daddy said. "You sure picked a good 'un."

John smiled and held out his hand.

I ran to him.

He scooped me up into his embrace, the long train of my gown swirling around us. I'd never ever in my life been so happy. Daddy was alive and I was marrying John Fant!

Then I woke up and realized it was all a foolish dream.

Chapter Three

I GOT SUNDAYS off, and after church the day was mine. The first month, I'd been busy settling in, but by the second month, I was ready to explore the town of Cupid. I'd met another maid at the First Methodist Church. Her name was Rosalie Smithe and she worked for the Farnsworths, who lived right next door to the McClearys. She was nineteen and from Pecos County. Just like me, she was the oldest of a big brood of kids, and we got on like a house afire.

As we were leaving church services the first Sunday in July, Rosalie asked me if I'd like to go with her to visit the Cupid Caverns.

"What's that?" I asked.

Her eyes grew wide like I was the dumbest thing she'd ever seen. "You've never heard of the Cupid Caverns?"

I shook my head.

"Oh, then you must come." She took my arm. "Go

home and change. I'll pack us a picnic basket and meet you in the town square in thirty minutes."

I was all excited to have made a new friend. Back home, there wasn't much time for idle activities and Mama had been real strict about what you could and couldn't do on the Lord's Day, but here there was no one to lecture me for not spending the day reading the Bible and reflecting on the grace of God. I felt a bit sinful as I put on my everyday clothes and ran to meet Rosalie.

Rosalie was a chatterbox, with long blond hair she kept plaited in a single braid down her back, just like I did. Her face was long, almost horsey, and her teeth seemed too big for her mouth, but she had a lively brown eyes and a pert little nose.

"You ever consider getting your hair cut like those flapper girls?" Rosalie asked, making scissor motions around her head.

I shrugged. "Never gave it much thought."

"Everybody back East is cutting their hair. Seems like it would be easier than plaiting up this mess every day. I'm thinkin' about doin' it. Whack it all off. Snip. Snip."

Suddenly, she had me wondering what it would be like to have short hair. "My mama says flappers are loose women."

"Your mama sounds judgmental."

That made me mad for a minute, but I didn't want to ruin the day, so I didn't say anything.

"Maybe she's just scared of her own womanly power." Rosalie tossed her head. "Women can vote now. We have rights."

"Not me," I said. "I just turned eighteen."

"Soon enough you can vote."

It seemed like an overwhelming responsibility. I knew nothing about politics. Maybe when the time came, if I was still working for Penelope, I'd ask John his opinion.

The day was hot as a firecracker and it wasn't long before we were sweating pretty good as we toiled up the incline leading from Cupid to the caverns. We took turns carrying the basket, first Rosalie, then me.

"It'll be cool in the caverns," Rosalie promised.

It took us almost an hour and a half to walk the six miles, and Rosalie prattled the whole time, filled me in on who was who in Cupid. All the rich folks lived on Stone Street, which fronted Lake Cupid. They had names like Fant and Van Zandt and Nielson and Farnsworth and McCleary.

The town had sprung up around the railroad as most West Texas towns had done. The small lake was an extra draw, a sweet oasis tucked in the valley of the Davis Mountains that jutted eight thousand feet above the town. The climate, cool misty mornings that burned off hot by afternoon, made for perfect wine growing, but because of Prohibition, the local vineyards had been forced to change to making grape juice instead of wine. Although Rosalie giggled and told me about rumors of bootleggers hiding the wine in a secret room inside the caverns.

I stared at her bug-eyed. "Is it safe to go into the caverns?"

"Aw sure." She waved a hand. "If there's bootleggers about, they're gonna know we're not revenuers."

Feeling excited by the prospect of meeting real bootleggers, but uneasy all the same, I cast a furtive glance over my shoulders, on the lookout for the criminal element, but saw nothing except the town of Cupid lying below.

We reached the entrance to the caverns, and immediately a blast of cool air greeted us.

"Do we just walk right on in?" I asked.

"Sure enough," Rosalie said.

"Who owns the property? Aren't we trespassing?"

"It's Fant land and you work for the Fants. Besides, it's in the works to turn the caverns over to the town to make it a city park. Everyone comes up here anyway. Might as well make it official."

Sounded reasonable to me.

Rosalie paused to take a flashlight from the picnic basket and switch it on. We both drank water from the Mason jar she'd packed, quenching our thirst after the long walk.

"Ready?" she asked.

A thrill ran through me. This was the most exciting thing I'd ever done. "Uh-huh."

We entered the cave.

It was darker than night, and without the flashlight I would have been scared to death. Rosalie shone the beam over the cavern walls. Wicked-looking rock formations spiked down from the ceiling like monster's teeth. At our feet were more daggered rocks, these sticking straight up. They were all different colors—orange, green, purple, white.

"Stalactites hang tight to the ceiling, stalagmites rise from the ground," Rosalie explained the difference.

"They look sharp and jabby."

"Keep to the path," Rosalie instructed. "And you don't have to worry about getting poked."

I gathered my skirt around me and stayed close behind her. Eerie silence surrounded us, broken only by sounds of stalactites dripping water onto the stalagmites and our tandem breathing echoing off the cave walls. The farther we went, the narrower the passages grew, the more my stomach churned. Was this what it was like to go down into the silver mine? Had my father felt this same edge of loneliness every single day of his life?

"Where are we going?" I asked.

"You'll see."

We twisted and turned as the path snaked through the crop of stalagmites, maneuvering through cave after cave until finally, we entered the last one. Rosalie paused and pushed the flashlight under her chin so that the beam spookily illuminated her face.

I shivered.

"Got the heebie-jeebies?"

"You look scary."

"You are about to see a miracle of the natural world," she said in a Barnum and Bailey voice. "Are you ready, Millie Greenwood?"

I nodded.

"I now give you . . ." Rosalie swung the beam of the flashlight away from her face and toward her left. "Cupid, the Roman god of erotic love."

I gasped at her shocking use of the word "erotic," but that was only the beginning of my surprise.

The stalagmite was over seven feet tall and almost touched the top of the ceiling of the small cave. The rock formation looked so much like Cupid standing on one leg, the other leg bent as if he were running, a quiver attached to his back and a cocked bow held in his hands loaded with an arrow ready to be flung.

I pressed a hand to my chest, awed beyond words.

"Ain't he somethin'?" Rosalie breathed.

He was indeed something, even though he didn't have a face, just a blob of greenish stone. I couldn't stop staring at it. "I can see where the town got its name."

"Worth the walk, wasn't it?"

It was.

"Wanna hear how Cupid got discovered?"

"Sure," I said, mesmerized past the point of being scared.

"Once upon a time, way back just after the Civil War, there was an outlaw on the run for horse thievin'."

"Sounds like an unsavory character."

"Oh no, Mingus Dill was a looker. Handsomer than John Fant."

"No one is handsomer than John Fant," I said staunchly.

"Mingus *was*."

"You can't prove that."

"Don't get all high behind about it."

"I'm sorry," I mumbled. "Go on about Mingus Dill."

"Legend has it he weren't really a horse thief, rather

he got caught barneymuggin' a sheriff's wife up in Fort Worth."

"Barneymugging?" I asked. "What's that?"

Rosalie let out a long-suffering sigh. "Don't you know anything?"

"I know a lot of stuff. Just not that."

"Barneymugging, you know . . . making love."

"Oh." My cheeks heated.

"Anyway, Mingus had to hightail it out the sheriff's bedroom window and stole his horse to get away. The sheriff got a posse together and they chased poor Mingus all the way to Jeff Davis County."

"That's a long way."

"Now about this same time," Rosalie went on. "This was before Cupid was founded, mind you, there were more women than men in Jeff Davis County, 'cause most every man of fightin' age had gone off to the Civil War."

"Except for outlaws."

"That's exactly right," Rosalie said. "So because of that, they made a rule around here that if any single woman in the county wanted to claim one of those outlaws, they could marry them and save them from being hung."

"That sounds like a strange custom."

"Nonetheless, it's true."

"The women must have been pretty desperate."

"Oh, they were. Especially Miss Louisa Hendricks. She was plain as an old mud fence, but she wanted a baby real bad."

"Poor Louisa."

"Life ain't fair sometimes. Mingus had heard about the

getting' married rule and these caverns so he came here to hide out. He didn't really want to get married, but if was he gonna get caught, then this was the place to get caught in."

I hung on her every word, completely enthralled with the tale.

"He pushed as deep into the cavern as he could and he ended up in this very room." Rosalie swung the flashlight over Cupid again for dramatic effect.

I tried to imagine it. Stumbling in here, the sheriff and his posse hot on your trail.

"Mingus heard the law crashing behind him, coming for him. There was no escape." Rosalie moved the beam from Cupid to shine it on the back of the cave wall. "As you can see, there's no other way out."

"What did he do?" I whispered.

"He fell down on his knees at the Cupid statue and he prayed like he was in church. Pleaded with Cupid to touch the heart of some kind local woman so she'd agree to marry him. And that's where he was when the sheriff found him."

"Did they hang him?"

"'Course not. This is a love story. Just when they was putting the noose around his neck, Louisa Hendricks stepped up and claimed him. The preacher married them on the spot."

"And they lived happily ever after?"

"They did indeed. They fell madly in love and it was all because of Cupid."

I took a deep breath. It was the most amazing story I'd ever heard.

"C'mon," Rosalie said. "It's time to get. We gotta long walk back."

I didn't want to go. I wanted to stay longer and think about Mingus and Louisa and the blasphemous magic of praying to Cupid, but Rosalie was right.

We left the caverns, blinking against the brightness of the afternoon sun. We were trying to decide where to eat our picnic when a brand-new Dagmar rolled to a stop outside the cavern entrance. Behind the wheel was a slick-looking man with a thin black mustache, Charlie Chaplin eyebrows, and a gray fedora. He honked the horn.

I took one look at him and my brain lit up: BOOTLEGGER.

"Hey tomatoes, wanna lift?" he invited.

I shook my head vigorously.

But Rosalie ran to the car. She had the picnic basket and she climbed into the seat beside him. "C'mon, Millie. Let's hitch a ride."

I shook my head. "I don't know this man."

"It's Buddy Grass, I went to school with his sister Gwynnie."

"I didn't."

Rosalie scooted across the seat and Buddy slipped his arm around her shoulder. A sneaky suspicion came over me. Had Rosalie set up this rendezvous with the bootlegger? Was he her secret boyfriend? Did they engage in barneymugging?

"Forget her," Buddy said. "We don't need no alarm clock anyways."

I scowled. "What's an alarm clock?"

"A chaperone." Rosalie tittered. "She's kinda dumb," she whispered loudly to Buddy.

"This isn't a good idea, Rosalie." I sank my hands on my hips.

"It'll be fine," she assured me. "We're just going for a drive."

"Well, doll?" Buddy Grass wriggled his Charlie Chaplin eyebrows. "You comin' or not?"

"Not."

"Fine by me. See ya, toots." Buddy put the car in gear and took off down the road, Rosalie stuck a hand out the window, waved good-bye.

Leaving me in a strange place, without anything to eat or drink, to walk home all by myself.

Feeling like the country rube I obviously was, I swallowed back the tears pushing into my throat. Dumb. Why did I have to be so dumb? I'd thought Rosalie wanted my company, but she'd just been using me as an excuse to meet up with Buddy Grass away from prying eyes.

I was hungry and thirsty and I'd never felt so alone.

Stop it. No wallowing in self-pity. I squared my shoulders and set my course for Cupid.

The sun beat down, baking my head, and I wished I'd worn a hat. My shoes kept slipping in the pebble-strewn path. I considered taking off my shoes and going barefooted, but the abundance of prickly cacti prevented me from doing that.

I'd walked no more than a quarter of a mile when there came the sounds of horse hooves trotting up behind me. Nervously, I wadded my hands into fists and cast a glance over my shoulder.

The sun was at the rider's back, casting his face in shadows, but he sat astride a magnificent palomino and I could see that he wore a cowboy hat, cowboy boots, and batwing chaps studded with silver conchos that glinted in the light.

My heart gave an odd little thump.

He reined in the horse a few yards away and swung down from the saddle.

I shaded my eyes with the edge of my hand but I still couldn't make out the man's features.

Spurs jangling, he strode toward me with long-legged, purposeful strides. That's when I spotted the gun holstered on his hips.

I gulped, swiped the sweat from my brow with the back of my hand. Who was he? What did he want with me? What should I do? Run? Hold my ground? I scanned the area—nothing but cactus, yucca, and scrub oak.

Nowhere to hide.

Nothing to do but face this head-on.

My chest tightened. I couldn't quite catch my breath. I steeled my body and raised my chin. "Hello."

"What are you doing way out here all by yourself, Millie?" drawled a familiar voice.

Blood that had earlier set my pulse racing was now pumping happy relief through my veins.

The cowboy was none other than John Fant.

Chapter Four

"I WAS OUT for a walk," I answered, not wanting to get Rosalie in trouble, although I wasn't sure why I was skirting the truth for her. She had abandoned me to my own devices to go off joyriding with a rumrunner. "I wanted to see the Cupid Caverns."

"All by yourself?"

Not wanting to tell a bald-faced lie, I didn't answer.

"And did you?" he asked, coming closer, a quirky smile on his lips. "See the caverns?"

"I did."

Up close, he was more handsome than ever in those cowboy clothes. I'd never seen him in a Stetson, boots, chaps, spurs, and gun. I couldn't forget the gun. I was fascinated by his transformation from business-suited executive to rangy cowpoke. Now I understood the calluses on his palms.

"Would you like a ride home?" he asked.

Ride on a horse behind John Fant? My entire body tingled at the thought.

"Where have you been on a Sunday?" I asked.

"Checking the herd."

"How often do you do that?"

"Every Sunday. I have a foreman that runs the spread, but I like getting my hands dirty."

"You work on Sunday?"

"Livestock has to eat seven days a week. Besides, I believe working is the best way to commune with God," he said. "What's more pious than an honest day's labor working with your hands?"

It was a different way of looking at things, a way that intrigued me. "Don't you ever take a day off?"

"Work settles my mind."

That I understood. "Where do you keep your horse in town?" I asked.

"There's a livery in Cupid. I board her there."

"What's her name?"

"Goldie."

"She's a pretty filly."

His gaze was fixed on my face. "That she is."

"I always wanted a horse of my own," I said wistfully. "All we had was an old Shetland pony for everyone to use."

"You want a ride into town, Miss Millie? It's a good six miles back to Cupid."

He hadn't meant anything by the invitation. Only being neighborly. Couldn't go daydreaming about things I could never have. "Thank you kindly. I will accept that ride."

He escorted me to his horse, climbed on, and then reached down a hand to help me swing up in the saddle behind him. His big hand held tight to my smaller one until I was safely in the seat.

"You might want to hold on," he said. "We're going down a steep grade."

I wrapped my arms around his waist. It felt too intimate with my breasts mashed up against his back, my legs on either side of his, my hands clasped over his chest, but I secretly thrilled to the closeness.

It was wrong, I know, but I couldn't help having a few fantasies. What would it feel like to kiss him? I'd never been kissed. Never been courted. There hadn't been much opportunity for it out in the hardscrabble sagebrush land where I'd been hatched. Cupid felt a million miles from where I'd come from, even though it was just a short distance south. It was a completely different planet.

I locked my fingers together and held on tight, felt the steady rise and fall of John's chest. Who knew that he would be so strong, his muscles so honed? His scent was honest, sunshine and leather and hard work. He did not smell of perfume as he had on the day I'd met him. I liked the contrast in him. He was both a man of the world and an ordinary cowboy. He could wear a fancy fragrance and six-shooters with equal ease. Not many people could straddle two worlds, but he made it look so easy.

"How are you liking Cupid?" he asked.

"Very much."

"My sister says you're a good worker."

"I appreciate the job." It was strange, having a conversation when I couldn't see his face. Impossible to gauge what he was thinking.

"How is your family?"

"They're doing well."

"Do you get homesick?"

"Not as much as I did at first."

"It's got to be hard, leaving your loved ones behind."

"You left your family behind when you went to the war," I pointed out.

"That's how I know it's hard."

"What was it like?" I asked.

"The war?"

"Uh-huh."

"Ugly," he said. "I don't like to talk about it."

Chastised, I shut my mouth.

"You're very brave," he said after a while. "I admire that about you."

He admired me! "I'm not," I argued.

"You propped your mother up after your father died."

"She was destroyed. My daddy was her one true love."

"One true love, huh?"

"Most people don't get that in their lifetime," I said. "They were very lucky."

"How do you know when someone is your one true love?"

"You feel it," I said, even though I had no personal experience of such a thing. "In every part of your being."

"And what exactly does that feel like?" He sounded completely amused.

"Heaven." I breathed.

"What does heaven feel like?"

"Home."

"So finding your one true love is like coming home?"

"Yes." I nodded even though he couldn't see. "Except better."

"How's that?"

"It's like coming home, Christmas, and your birthday all rolled into one and it lasts a lifetime."

"Tall order for anyone."

"But worth holding out for."

"Is that what you're doing, Millie?" he said softly. "Holding out for one true love?"

"I don't know," I answered honestly.

"You don't know if you going to wait to find your one true love?"

"I don't know if I *want* to find my one true love."

"Why not? It sounds wonderful, coming home, Christmas, your birthday all rolled into one and the feeling lasts a lifetime."

"Because," I said, "when you lose that love, the way my mother did, it's the worst pain in the world."

"Are you saying a lifetime of loving isn't worth the pain?"

"I don't know," I admitted. "But it scares me."

We said nothing else for a while as Goldie picked her way over the rocky trail. Gravity pulled me forward in the seat, a natural slide closer to John, and then I did the most daring thing imaginable.

I rested my cheek against his back.

My audacity shocked me, but I did not move my head.

Just rested my ear against him, and listened to the steady beating of his heart, my fingers still interlaced in front of his ribs.

I held my breath, waiting to see how he would react. I wasn't the only one full of surprises.

John placed a hand over mine, his calloused thumb rubbed across my knuckles; a comforting touch to be sure, but it also aroused feelings deep inside me. Feelings I'd been struggling to suppress for weeks.

My skin tingled. My heart was a trapped dove inside my chest, fluttering and flapping. Way down low, I felt a feminine stirring. A stirring that I could not name, but it was an overwhelming, primal force, urgent and demanding. I wanted to dance and sing and laugh and cry. I wanted to both praise God and do all manner of sin with this man.

But it was a tenuous thrill and I well and truly knew it. I would be no Ruthie, no matter how much I might want to lie down with John and give my body over to him. And it wasn't because I was a good girl, although I usually tried hard to be one.

Rather, my restraint arose from the huge class chasm between us. He was a rich man at the top of the heap, the king of the Trans-Pecos, and I was nothing more than a maid at best. At worst, I was simply the pity-case daughter of a man who'd been killed in one of his mines. I understood my place in the world and it was not with a man like John Fant.

The problem was that with John dressed like a cowboy, the lines between us blurred. For a few minutes, it was easy to pretend that he was just a lonesome cowpoke, raised on the land, not so different from me. He even smelled familiar, like Jeff Davis County earth. Home. He smelled like home.

For a dangerous stretch of time, I foolishly let myself dream.

We rode like that for several minutes, not speaking, just being there together in the saddle.

"Millie," he said after a while.

My eyes were closed and I was concentrating on listening to the beating of his heart and absorbing the heat from his body and marveling how good it felt to be so close to him. I knew this moment couldn't last and I was milking it for everything it was worth. "Uh-huh."

"I've made a decision."

"About what?" I murmured.

"The mine."

"Are you going to close it?"

"I'm going to repair the mine and keep it open."

"Even though it will cost you more money than you can get back out of it?"

"Yes," he said. "It's the right thing to do."

I squeezed him tight, letting him know how much that meant to me.

He chuckled. "Ease up a bit, I need to breathe."

Embarrassed, I dropped my arms.

"You can still hang on," he said. "Don't want you to fall, Millipede."

Millipede! He'd given me a nickname.

We were long past the rocky incline, on the flat

ground of the valley floor; there was no need for me to keep hanging on tight, but I did it anyway. Sliding my arms around him, feeling his warmth seep through me all over again.

Millipede. He'd called me Millipede.

A grin spread over my face bigger than Texas. This was the most romantic thing that had ever happened to me.

But my grin quickly faded away. This was also the most wretched thing, because even though I could never say the words out loud, I realized something that my heart had known since that day on my daddy's porch.

John Fant was my one true love and there was no way in the whole wide world that we could ever be together.

AFTER OUR HORSEBACK ride, I didn't see John again for an entire month. By day, he filled my thoughts. By night, he ransacked my dreams and I'd awake achy and restless.

Finally, I worked up the courage to ask Mabel about his absence.

"Oh, he's out at the Fant Oil Field in Pecos County. They're drilling a new well and he's helping to get it started." She narrowed her eyes at me. "Why are you asking?"

I shrugged. "Just noticed he hadn't been around lately. That's all."

Mabel's frown deepened. "Well, stop noticing. His comings and goings are not the business of a maid. Now wash out those Mason jars. We're canning tomatoes today."

It was late August and miserable hot. That's one thing I hate about gardening. The crops come due at the hottest part of the year and you have to fire up the stoves for canning. Mabel had all the windows raised and the electric ceiling fan whirling, but it didn't do anything except stir the heat.

Right in the big middle of canning, when Mabel and I had every surface in the kitchen covered with either tomatoes, tomato skin peelings, Mason jars, or vats of boiling water, Mrs. Bossier strolled in.

"My Lord, it's hot in here," Penelope said, fanning herself with a copy of *Harper's Bazaar* that the postman had delivered that very morning.

"Canning, ma'am," Mabel said.

"I can see that," Penelope said a bit peevishly, scooted a basket of tomatoes off a kitchen chair, and set them on the floor, before flopping down to where the tomatoes had just been.

"Is there something you need, ma'am?" Mabel asked. "Glass of ice cold water?"

"Indeed."

Mabel snapped a finger at me and pointed to the icebox. I turned to fetch the glass of ice water.

"I'm in charge of the Ladies' League charity event this year and I'm all out of ideas. I can't think of a theme that hasn't been done to death." Penelope picked up a kitchen towel and dabbed the sweat from her forehead.

"I thought you were through with that bunch," Mabel said, screwing the lids down tight on a batch of canned tomatoes she was readying for the boiling water.

"One can never be free from charity responsibilities and this is my opportunity to redeem my family name."

"You didn't do nothing to ruin the family name," Mabel said. "It was all Ruthie's fault."

Penelope clucked her tongue. "What did I tell you about mentioning that girl's name in this house?"

Mabel pantomimed like she was locking her lips shut and throwing the key away over her shoulder.

I set the glass of water down in front of Mrs. Bossier.

"Thank you, Millie." She smiled at me, but I couldn't help feeling she was comparing me to the infamous Ruthie.

And to tell the truth, I was feeling a sad kinship with the Bossiers' unfortunate former maid, loving a man she could never have.

Penelope sipped her water and leafed through the magazine. What was she doing hanging out in the kitchen?

Mabel met my gaze, shrugged, and inclined her head toward the stove. Message received. Get back to work.

I was snagging blanched tomatoes from the hot water with a slotted spoon and dumping them into a bowl of cold water so I could peel the skin right off them after they cooled down, when Penelope let out a whoop.

Mabel and I both jumped and turned back to see what had made her squawk.

Penelope was on her feet doing a little dance and flapping the page of *Harper's Bazaar* around.

"You okay, Mrs. Bossier?" Mabel asked.

"I've got it! I've got it?"

The way she was dancing, I was wondering if she had chiggers.

Mabel pushed a damp strand of gray hair from her forehead with the back of her hand, wiped her hands on her apron, and went over to Penelope. "What is it?"

"The theme of the Ladies' League charity event. It's right here in *Harper's Bazaar.* They're all the rage on the East Coast." She thumped the page. "We're going to hold a dance marathon."

Mabel took the magazine from her, read the article about dance marathons. Fascinated, I peered over her shoulder to read it for myself and discovered that dance marathons for charity required the contestants to get sponsors to pay them for the length of time they danced, say a penny an hour. The marathon continued until there was only one couple left dancing.

"Not only am I going to put on the dance marathon, but I'm going to dance it and earn the most money for charity, and then those old biddies on the Ladies' League will have to stop turning their noses up at over that unfortunate incident with that unfortunate girl."

Mabel eyed Penelope. "How you aimin' on doing that?"

Penelope placed a palm over her heart. "I'll have you know, I was one of the best dancers at Oldfields Finishing School, second only to my best friend, Wallis."

"Her best friend was a boy?" I whispered to Mabel.

"Wallis is a girl with a boy's name," Mabel whispered back.

Penelope was waltzing about the room, bumping into

bushel baskets full of tomatoes. "Her first name is Bessie, but she hates it. Wallis has such a strong personality. The name suits her much better than Bessie."

"I wasn't talking about your dancing abilities." Mabel steered her back on topic. "I was speaking of Mr. Beau. That man has two left feet."

"True, Beau would rather have his head stuck in a tin can than get out on the dance floor." Penelope sighed. "And we're all better for his lack of interest. John will be my partner. He's the best dancer in Cupid."

At the mention of John's name my pulse quickened. He knew how to dance too? Was there anything the man could not do?

Mabel shook her head. "Mr. John doesn't have time to practice with you. Not with rebuilding the silver mine and bringing in that new well."

Penelope paused, momentarily stumped. "You're right. I need someone to practice with. I don't know the new dances at all." She eyed me speculatively. "Millie, do you know how to dance?"

"I can square dance, ma'am."

"I suppose you'll do. We start practicing tomorrow. I'm going to go call Wallis and see if she's got any tips."

With that, she waltzed away.

Mabel let out a long held breath, shook her head. "I don't envy you."

"Why's that?" I asked.

"When Penelope gets an idea in her head, she's like a bulldog with a bone. Mark my word. She'll dance the legs right off of you."

Chapter Five

Penelope's friend Wallis Simpson was sending a dance marathon promoter from Chicago out to Cupid to orchestrate the event, and she was over the moon. More than once, Penelope said, "I'm going to show those old biddies. We're going to put on a dance unlike anything the Trans-Pecos has ever seen."

The Ladies' League charity event was always held the last weekend in September. That gave us six weeks to practice, and Mabel's prediction was indeed prophetic. Penelope and I danced three to four hours a day. Danced until our legs were so achy and sore that we often woke in the middle of the night with painful charley horses.

When I'd protest that I wasn't getting all my cleaning done, Penelope would wave away my complaints. "This is more important than a few cobwebs in the corner."

Margaret Fant watched her grandchildren, keeping the kids from getting underfoot while we practiced. I appreciated how this family worked together and supported each other, but it made me homesick for my own kin.

We learned every single one of the hot new dance crazes sweeping the cities from a chart that Penelope's friend Wallis sent us—the Charleston, the fox-trot, and the Baltimore Buzz. I was surprised at how quickly I picked up the steps, and Penelope declared me a natural dancer. When I danced I felt freer than I'd ever felt in my life. Dance took me out of myself and into the music spilling from Penelope's Victrola.

"You have an elegant grace," she said. Flattered, I blushed, until she added, "That you rarely see in someone from your station in life."

There it was. The unbridgeable gulf between her class and mine. She might use me as a stand-in dance partner, but I would never be her equal. I knew that, but it still stung.

The closer it got to the dance marathon, the more Penelope pushed me, and we'd finish our dance sessions exhausted, but exhilarated.

"I'm going to set this town on fire!" Penelope declared, and rubbed her palms together.

"Will Mr. Fant know these dances?" I asked Penelope, not daring to say John's first name. I was careful to look away from her when I asked the question, so she couldn't see from my eyes how I felt about her brother. I didn't want to lose my job.

"John is a man of the world," she said. "He gets to Houston quite often and I know for a fact he's been to some of the jazz clubs there. I'm sure some of the young ladies have taught him a thing or two."

Jealousy made my stomach hurt. I didn't like thinking about John dancing with other women. Silly of me, I know, but I could no more stop the jealousy than I could stop breathing.

"Maybe you should practice with him this last week before the dance marathon," I broached the subject carefully. My reasoning was selfish. I wanted John in Penelope's house.

"I've already asked. He's says he can't make any promises, but he'll try to get in a practice session or two before the event."

My hopes leaped. I saw John around town of course—at church or in passing on the street. He'd smile and lift his hat, but he'd never stop for a lingering conversation. Whenever I hung out the clothes, I'd peeked over the clothesline, but I never again caught him smoking his pipe. I assumed he'd given up the habit. I wondered if he'd already forgotten our ride home from the caverns. Or that he'd nicknamed me Millipede.

Penelope had ordered a flapper dress all the way from Chicago. It arrived on Friday, the day before the dance marathon, and John was the one to bring it into the house.

There was a knock on the door and I opened it to find John standing there with the package in his hand.

"I intercepted the delivery," he explained.

I lowered my lashes and stepped aside. "Please, do come in."

"Is that my dress?" Penelope came running into the room like she was the same age as my sister Jenny, her face alight, her hands grabbing for the package.

"Don't I even get a kiss on the cheek, dear sister?" John asked, sweeping off his Panama hat and hanging it on the hook by the front door, where it rested beside Mr. Bossier's newsboy cap. "I put aside everything to come dance with you."

Instead of a kiss on the cheek, Penelope lightly punched his upper arm. "That's for not coming to practice before now."

"Ow." John pretended she'd hurt him and rubbed his arm. "Relax. In a dance marathon, you don't have to be a great dancer. You just have to have a lot of physical stamina. The point is to outlast the other dancers, not outshine them."

"I intend on doing both."

"I'm sure you will," he told her.

"Wait here. I'm going to go try on the dress." With the package tucked under her arm, she bounded up the stairs to the bedroom she shared with Mr. Bossier.

"Wow," John said to me. "I had no idea she was this invested in the dance marathon."

"Oh, she's very invested." I nodded.

"I've heard you've been my stand-in," he said.

I finally dared to sneak a peek at his face. "No one could ever stand in for you."

He laughed at that. A clever sound that made me smile. "You'll be forever ruined for dancing with a man."

"What do you mean?" I asked, alarmed. Many of my fantasies were centered on dancing with John and even though they were just fantasies, the thought of being ruined scared me to death.

"After this, you'll always try to lead."

I put a hand to my forehead "My goodness, you're right. Mrs. Bossier taught me to lead."

"But what's wrong with that?" he asked with a wink. "Women now have the right to vote, they should have the right to lead if they wish."

"I don't want to lead," I said, not wanting him to think I was manly.

"Everyone," Penelope called downstairs. "Gather around so you can witness my grand entrance."

John and I grinned at each other and in unison we moved to the bottom of the stairs. I marveled at how we fell into step together, side by side.

Mabel came from the kitchen, wiping her hands on her apron and smelling of vanilla. "What's all the fuss about?"

John waved with a flourish to the top of the stairs where Penelope had appeared.

She stood on the landing, posing with a dramatic flair in the stunning mint green dress. It was sleeveless, quite scandalous indeed for the likes of Cupid, and it had a straight loose bodice that dropped all the way to her hips. The hem hit her just a few inches below her knees, exposing lots of leg adorned in silk stockings. On her feet, she wore high-heeled shoes, and on her head sat a floppy mint green hat decorated with white lilies of the valley.

"My heavens," Mabel muttered, "The world is turning topsy-turvy."

I stared at Penelope, awestruck. She could have stepped straight off the pages of *Harper's Bazaar.* Until this dancing thing, I had tended to think of Mrs. Bossier as matronly. She was well and properly married and had two children, but right now, she looked no older than I. Her passion for dancing shone like a beacon from her eyes.

No way would I dare tell her that when she appeared at the Ladies' League event dressed like this, whether she earned hundreds of dollars for the charity or not, she would not regain her lost position with that tight-lipped crowd. In fact, appearing dressed this way might be her social undoing.

I wondered why John did not point this out, but I shouldn't have been surprised. I'd already noticed he wasn't the type to put restrictions on the behavior of others. Which was better? Warning his sister of her potential downfall or giving Penelope her independence and allowing her to make her own mistakes? I'd grown up in a world marked by distinct right or wrong. This gray area confused me.

"You would look amazing in that dress, Millie," John murmured so low that I was certain I had misunderstood him, but I couldn't stop a sweet thrill from sweeping over me.

Penelope spread her arms wide. "Ta-da."

John cupped his curled fingers over his mouth as if he were speaking through a megaphone and said, "Here she is folks, straight from Chicago, to grace our modest hamlet with her incredible dancing skills, the thoroughly modern Miss Penny."

In that moment I saw them as they must have been as children, loving and teasing each other.

"Oh, John, you're making fun," Penelope protested, but her cheeks turned a dark shade of pink and she started walking sideways down the stairs, regal in her flapper clothes. She was the bravest woman I knew, daring to do something most women wouldn't have the courage to pursue.

And that's when one of Penelope's high heels slipped out from under her and sent her plunging down the length of the stairs.

ALL THREE OF us ran to Penelope; John and I, being younger and quicker, beat Mabel to her side.

But Mabel, being bigger and older, muscled us away. She knelt on the floor, scooped Penelope up in her plump arms, and cradled her back in the crook of her elbow. "Good Lord, ma'am, what on earth was you thinkin'? Parading down the steps in those heels."

Concern pulled John's lips tight. "Sister, are you okay?"

Tears sprang to Penelope's eyes and she grabbed for her ankle. "Ow, ow, ow."

I looked down at her right ankle that was swelling big

as a cow's udder, and plastered my hand over my mouth.

Penelope's gaze met mine. "It's not that bad, is it?"

I shook my head.

Penelope reached for John's arm. "Get me to my feet. I have to see if I can stand."

"Penny, that's not a good idea."

"Johnny," she said through clenched teeth. "Help me up."

Reluctantly, he took one of her arms and Mabel took the other and they helped Penelope to her feet, but the second she put weight on that right leg, she collapsed back onto the floor with a loud wail of pain.

Mabel clucked her tongue. "There'll be no marathon dancing for you."

Beneath the pallor of her skin, Penelope burst into fresh tears. "No," she whispered, "I have to dance."

But I could see the fight draining out of her.

"I've bragged to the Ladies' League." She sniffled. "I have to show them up."

"Well, you know what they say about pride going before a fall," John said.

"You're not helping. I was going to raise the most money for needy children. It was my way back into everyone's good graces after that mess with Ruthie."

"I don't know why you care so much about what a lot of old biddies think." Mabel fussed over her, dabbed Penelope's tears with the corner of her apron.

"They can make or break you, Mabel. Success in life comes down to how well you play politics." Penelope let out a long sigh, leaned back against the wall, and closed her eyes. Her right leg was stuck out in front of her, her left knee drawn up.

Mabel carefully rearranged the flapper dress to cover as much of Penelope's leg as possible. "There now."

"Shoo." Penelope waved her away. "Let me think."

Mabel got to her feet and waddled to the door. "I'll go for the doctor."

I nibbled on my bottom lip and glanced over at John. He studied me with a pensive expression in his eyes. Did I have something on my face? I scrubbed a palm over my cheek.

"Have you registered for the marathon yet?" he asked his sister.

Penelope waved a weak hand, but kept her eyes closed. "The registration starts tomorrow morning. Why?"

"In the rules and regulations brochure that you gave me to study, it said that once the contestants have registered, if one partner drops out the other one can't go on with another partner."

Penelope opened one eye. "What are you getting at?"

"If you haven't registered us yet, I can still dance and uphold the family name."

She perked up a little. "With whom? Elizabeth is still in Baltimore and besides, even if she was here, Elizabeth might be a good dancer but she has no stamina. A dance marathon is about more than just dancing. It's being able to outlast everyone else. You're not going to find anyone who fits that bill this late date."

Who was Elizabeth? I darted a sidelong glance at John. An old girlfriend? My chest tightened and I felt slightly sick at my stomach.

John was looking straight at me. "You're wrong about that."

Penelope's other eye popped open. "You don't mean—"

"Who else has been practicing for weeks?" he asked.

I frowned. Were they talking about what I thought they were talking about?

"It's unheard of, John." Penelope swept the flapper hat off her head and fanned herself with it. One of the lilies of the valley flew off and landed on the floor at my feet.

"This is a new decade, Pen, things are changing."

"But what will everyone say?" she mused.

"That Mrs. Penelope Fant Bossier has set this town on its ear."

"It would be social suicide."

"Or you could start your own society of younger, more modern women."

Penelope canted her head pensively. "What about you?"

"I don't give a damn what they think about me. Let's shake this place up."

I widened my eyes. I'd never heard him curse. He must be serious.

Penelope moved to sit up straighter; her faint smile couldn't cover her wrench of pain. "You make an excellent point, little brother."

Both of them were staring at me now.

"She is about my size. The dress would fit her."

Gooseflesh speckled my arms. I looked from John to Penelope and back again.

Penelope notched her chin up and gave John her permission when she said recklessly, “Why not?”

“What is it? What are you talking about?” But I knew and I could scarcely believe it. Didn’t want to believe it, because it was an unreal dream. Too late, hope spread through me as bright and yellow as the noonday sun.

“Millie,” John said. “Will you be my partner for the dance marathon?”

Chapter Six

THE DANCE MARATHON started at noon on Saturday in the Cupid High School gymnasium. John had registered us for the contest that morning, and when he came to the house, he brought me a white corsage that matched the lilies of the valley on the floppy green hat.

"Oh, John," I whispered as if he'd actually come to pick me up for a date. "It's beautiful." By the end of the marathon the flower would wilt, just as we would, but in the moment I was enchanted.

"Here," he said. "Let me put it on for you."

He ducked his head and leaned over me, his fingers grazing my skin as he expertly pinned the corsage to my dress just below my left shoulder. No fumbling, no hesitation. This man knew how to pin a corsage.

"It's my first corsage," I admitted.

"It won't be your last," he said so convincingly that I believed him. "You'll soon have boyfriends swarming around you."

I didn't want boyfriends swarming around me. I only wanted John. What a foolish dreamer I was!

Maybe so, but today, the dream was all mine.

Penelope had spent the night on the sofa in the parlor because she couldn't make it up the stairs with her swollen ankle. The doctor had come by previous afternoon and diagnosed it as a severe sprain. She was sitting on the sofa with her foot propped up on an ottoman. Addie sat on the floor in front of her while Penelope braided her daughter's hair.

"You look boo-de-ful, Millie," Addie proclaimed.

"Why thank you, Miss Addie." I curtsied for her and she giggled.

Even Mr. Bossier came into the room to see what was going on. He had young Ernest on his shoulders, and the chubby-cheeked toddler was tugging on his hair. "Why Millie," Beau said. "You're going to make the other girls at the dance jealous."

My faced heated and I ducked my head. I felt so scandalous in Penelope's mint green dress. Just like a daring flapper. And when John held out his elbow for me to take his arm, I almost swooned.

"Win that trophy for me, Millie!" Penelope said, looking wistful.

"I'll do my best."

"Beau is going to borrow a wheelchair from the hospital," Penelope said. "So I can come watch. We'll be there later today to cheer you on. Mother and Father are coming with us too."

For a moment, I felt like I was one of them. Not merely

a maid, but a proper member of the household. I had no idea, at the time, how dangerous such a notion could be.

John escorted me to his Nash roadster and I went from feeling like a flapper to part of the family to a regal queen as I slid across those cushy seats. When we got to the high school I was amazed to see all the vehicles. More than what was usually parked in front of the church on Sunday morning. Penelope's dance marathon was off to a great start.

Over the entrance to the gymnasium was a big sign: "Dance Marathon Today. 25¢ Admission for Spectators." Then below it, in smaller letters, was another sign that read: "All proceeds go to the Ladies' League Charity Fund." Off to one side of the gymnasium, a first aid tent had been set up where nurses in white stood at the ready with rolls of bandages and bottles of Mercurochrome.

I'd never seen anything like this. I was a simple country girl from Whistle Stop. I shifted my weight on the balls of my feet, shuffling from side to side as we waited in line to get in. My toes were moving around a little too much in Penelope's high heels. They were a half size too big and I'd stuffed paper in the back of them.

John put a hand on my shoulder. "Nervous?"

If I wasn't before, his touch cinched it. I gulped. Nodded.

From inside the building came the sound of the band tuning up by running through a quick medley of songs, and six weeks of training took over. My toes automatically started tapping.

"Your eyes glow when you're happy," John murmured.

He was right. I was happy. More than happy. I was over the moon to be here with John. Soon we would be dancing. Touching. For hours and hours on end.

We checked in and received numbers. Volunteers pinned them to our backs. John and I were couple number 12.

"My lucky number," John said.

The gymnasium was a hubbub of excitement. There were more people here than in the entire population of my hometown. Couples took to the dance floor to await the official noon start of the marathon. Spectators climbed to find seats on the bleachers. The band was set up on the stage at the back of the gym. On the opposite end of the building, long tables had been erected and they were loaded with refreshments. The smell of strong coffee and popcorn wafted in the air.

Rosalie was on the dance floor with Buddy Grass. They were couple number 30. She wriggled her fingers at me. We hadn't spoken more than a handful of words to each other since the day she abandoned me at the caverns. I didn't hold a grudge. Because of her, I'd gotten to ride on the back of Goldie behind John. She was the one who'd avoided me. Embarrassed about her behavior, I guessed.

I blew out a deep breath, rubbed my damp palms down the outside of my thighs.

"You're going to do fine," John lowered his head to whisper, his breath warm and tickly against my ear.

To distract myself, I counted the contestants. Fifty-five couples in all. A few minutes before the clock struck twelve, the promoter got up on stage. Using a bright yellow megaphone, he introduced himself, talked about the Ladies' League charity, and then explained the rules. "For the next twenty-four hours you will be dancing. If only one couple is left on the dance floor before noon tomorrow, the dance marathon will be over at that time."

"What if there's more than one couple left by noon tomorrow," someone called out.

"Then the marathon will continue until there is just one couple remaining."

"What if that takes days?" someone else asked.

"Then it takes days."

That sent a murmur rippling through the crowd. My own pulse did a ripple of its own.

The promoter went on. "All couples must remain touching at all times. Failure to maintain physical contact results in automatic disqualification. There will be spotters on the sidelines making sure the dancers stay in body contact the entire time."

The crowd tittered.

It was a scandalous thought. Constant physical contact with a man who was not even my boyfriend. A man I was secretly in love with. I could hardly breathe.

John reached over to take my hand.

My heart thumped crazily.

We were joined now, until the end of the marathon, or we were disqualified.

"All couples must remain moving at all times," the promoter continued. "You can sway, but you cannot stop. If you stop, you're automatically disqualified."

I was so pepped up with energy and promise I couldn't imagine that not moving would be a problem. Even now I was fidgeting, anxious to get started.

"Every two hours there will be a ten-minute break. When you hear this horn . . ." He honked a loud horn and everyone jumped. "It's the start of your ten-minute break. It will be honked a second time after nine minutes, indicating you should return to the dance floor. If you haven't returned at the ten-minute mark, at which time the band will begin again, you will be disqualified. Any questions?"

No one said anything.

The promoter eyed the clock mounted on the wall above the gymnasium door and nodded toward the band. "Ready, set . . . dance!"

The band launched into the Charleston.

We were off.

Except that the Charleston is a difficult dance to complete while touching your partner throughout. A quarter of the contestants were disqualified during that first dance.

But John was smart, the minute the band struck the first notes of the Charleston, he whispered, "Never let go of my hand."

And I didn't.

We flew through the next six hours, with those short breaks every two hours, swinging from one dance to the next. The beads on my flapper dress made soft little clacking noises as they tapped together as we spun, twirled, and whirled. It was exhilarating in the same way as galloping on a spirited horse across the desert flats, but this was better because the whole time, John and I were touching.

It was magical. A day to remember forever. We were so attuned to each other. The way we moved together you would have thought we'd been dancing partners for years. I barely even noticed the blisters starting to rub on the sides of my pinky toes from the too-big shoes.

On and on we danced.

Others around us were wilting, but John and I bloomed.

The third horn sounded and while we were slightly winded, we were both feeling strong and ready for more. Penelope, Beau, Addie, Ernest, and John's parents were in the stands cheering us on. John took off his jacket and I doffed the floppy hat and we gave them to Penelope for safekeeping.

We drank a cup of coffee and wolfed down chicken salad sandwiches for energy and then we were back on the dance floor again for "Nobody's Sweetheart."

John's fingers were laced through mine.

My chest fisted. I wasn't anybody's sweetheart, but how I wanted to be John's! *Dreaming, Millie. You're too sensible for that.*

A sigh escaped my lips.

"What is it?" John asked, his gaze swallowing my face.

I shook my head.

"Come on." John winked and twirled me. "You can tell me."

I ducked my head, and did not answer.

"Tell me your secrets, Millie," John coaxed.

I shrugged and stepped forward.

"You're trying to lead."

"Your sister's fault."

He laughed. "So, you're not going to tell me why you were sighing?"

"It's nothing."

"Then why not tell me?"

"You'll think I'm foolish." I dared to meet his dark eyes. They looked like simmering pots of melted chocolates. The room was suddenly far too hot.

"Never."

"I feel like Cinderella."

His smile was tender. "Have you ever been to a dance?"

"Not like this." I waved my hand. "Square dances."

"I don't think you're foolish."

"I know it's silly, but it's my one special night. If your sister hadn't hurt her ankle I wouldn't be here."

John lowered his head to mine. "Shh, don't tell anybody this."

"What?"

"This isn't very nice of me, but I consider it a happy coincidence that she hurt her ankle. If she hadn't, I wouldn't have had the pleasure of dancing with *you*."

My body heated all over. I couldn't believe that John Fant was saying these things to me.

"I'll tell you something else." His voice was so low I could scarcely hear him above the music.

"What's that?" I whispered.

"I feel a bit like Prince Charming with you in my arms. It is one special evening."

The band picked that moment to start playing "It Had to Be You."

John's eyes hooked to mine.

Mesmerized, I stared back, unable to look away. What if? What if? What if? The question beat through my temple. But hope is a dangerous thing and I didn't have the courage to crush it out.

"You're different from any girl I've ever met." John lowered his eyelids and peered at me through thick black lashes.

"In what way?"

"You're quite sensible for one so young. Naive to be sure, but underneath it, you have a surprising capacity to quickly grasp reality."

I canted my head, not sure if this was a compliment or not.

"You don't seem to care about frivolous things," he went on.

"That's because I come from a poor family," I said. "You're accustomed to society women, who have the time and money to worry about frivolous things."

"Society women don't have a market on frivolousness," he said.

"What do you mean?"

"Maids can be just as frivolous. For instance the young maid who works for the Farnsworths. She's making a big mistake dating Buddy Grass."

"Who says Rosalie is dating him?" I asked. "Just because they're dancing together."

"True enough," he conceded. "But I see the way she looks at him."

The same way I looked at John? I quickly glanced over at Rosalie and Buddy so he wouldn't see the stark desire on my face for something I could not have. "Is Buddy Grass a bootlegger?"

"You're not interested in him yourself, are you?" John sounded alarmed.

"No." Couldn't John see that I only had eyes for him?

"Stay away from the likes of Buddy Grass," he growled. "He's no good."

Was he jealous? My heart flip-flopped and I couldn't stop a smile from plucking at the corners of my lips.

Many of the spectators had gone home to their dinners, including the Fants and Bossiers. The bleachers were less than half full now and the dancers had dwindled to thirty-two couples. Rosalie and Buddy Grass were among them. We were still a long way from claiming the prize.

Twilight pushed the sun from the windows of the gymnasium. We were all moving slower now, shuffling instead of lively high stepping. The band members had changed out, bringing in fresh musicians at the last break. The Ladies' League volunteers had switched out too.

"May I ask you a question, Millie?" John asked.

"I'm not going anywhere."

"What were your hopes and dreams for the future before your father died?"

I shrugged. "Same as anybody else, I guess. Get married one day, have children."

"Nothing more?"

"What else is there?"

"No big dreams? No secret fantasy that you've never told anyone?"

Oh yes. "There's dreams, Mr. Fant," I said, "and then there's reality."

He looked amused. "We're back to Mr. Fant? I thought we got over that a long time ago."

"There's only so many options for the daughter of a silver miner with seven kids. No sense setting yourself up for heartbreak." *Go ahead. Tell it like you believe it.* Too late. It was too late not to set myself up for heartbreak. I was already there.

"You're smart as a whip, Millie Greenwood, you could be anything you want. A teacher. A nurse. A shop owner."

Smart. He'd called me smart. "Those things cost money."

"If you wanted to go to school, I'd be happy to send you."

"Mr. Fant, you don't owe me just because my daddy died in your mine."

"That's not the way I'm looking at it."

"Isn't it?"

"No."

"I wouldn't be here if the mine hadn't caved in."

He didn't say anything. What could he say? It was true enough. I wished I hadn't been so blunt, but I had to do something to make him hush. I couldn't keep dreaming impossible dreams.

The promoter took the stage, brought that yellow megaphone to his mouth. It was ten minutes until the next break. "Attention, dancers. It's time for the Runaround. When the band starts playing 'Rhapsody in Blue,' grab your partner's hand and start running clockwise around the gym. When the music stops, the last five couples will be eliminated, so you have to hurry, hurry, hurry."

The band struck "Rhapsody in Blue."

John looked at me and I looked at him and in unison we yelled, "Run."

We took off, sprinting ahead of everyone else.

It was hard enough dancing in high-heeled shoes that were half a size too big for you, but running in them was a whole other story. But we'd beaten everyone else to the punch and we were leading the pack of runners sprinting around the gym. It was a wild and crazy free-for-all.

One girl tripped and went falling, breaking contact with her partner. A spotter from the sidelines blew a whistle and they were out. John tightened his grip on me. "If you go down, I go down."

"I think my lungs are about to explode." I chuffed.

"You can do it, Millipede."

His nickname for me!

A couple was pulling up close behind us. John and I exchanged glances.

"You're as competitive as I am, aren't you, Millie Greenwood?" he asked.

"You bet."

He winked. "Let's show them how it's done."

I kicked off those high-heeled shoes and they went flying as John and I ran as fast as we could to outpace the couple behind us.

Just when I thought I could not take one step farther, the horn blew, signaling the break.

The last five groaning couples were disqualified.

Laughing, John and I collapsed onto the floor, along with everyone else.

We looked at each other and we could not stop laughing. It felt so good to laugh with him on the gymnasium floor. It was so unorthodox, so improper, but all for a good cause, so who could complain, right?

That's when I realized my dress had risen up, exposing my knees and the garter holding up the stockings. There was a run in stockings as well, but John's eyes were locked on my legs like they were the prettiest things he'd ever seen.

My cheeks burned and I yanked at the skirt of the dress, pulling it down past my knees. But it was too late. He'd already seen my knees. If my mother could see me now. She'd be shocked and give me a stern lecture about propriety.

"Your toes are bleeding," John exclaimed.

And before I knew what he was doing, he got to his feet and scooped me up into his arms.

"What are you doing?"

"Taking care of you."

"It's not your place. Put me down."

"Hush," he said sweetly and carried me outside into the cool night air. Someone had held the door open for us and John marched straight for the first aid tent.

A nurse bustled over. "Set her down."

John settled me onto a cot.

On the cot beside me, the girl that had tripped earlier was having Mercurochrome dabbed on her skinned knee by another nurse. It seemed a night for exposed knees.

The nurse clicked her tongue over my blistered toes and set about salving and dressing them.

"Do you want to call it quits?" John asked.

"No." I shook my head vehemently. "How much time to do we have left in the break?"

He glanced at his pocket watch. "Five minutes."

"Could you please hurry up?" I asked the nurse.

"You're going back in there?" She gave me a disapproving look.

"I am."

"Wrap her feet up good," John instructed.

"There's no time for that," I said. "I need a ladies' room break."

"You go for that," he said. "I'll grab us some sandwiches and meet you back on the dance floor."

Hobbled by my bandaged feet, I barely made it back to the dance floor in time. One second more and we would have been out. Eight hours in and we were down to twenty-six couples.

We danced and ate sandwiches—peanut butter this time—not even bothering with dance steps, just moving our feet. I couldn't believe we had another sixteen hours to go.

"I'm beginning to think your sister is a sadist," I said.

"I'm inclined to agree."

"Do you think she fell down the stairs on purpose to avoid this torture?"

"I wouldn't be surprised."

"I think she got the better of the deal. She's riding around in a wheelchair."

"Prima donna," he teased.

A spasm grabbed the calf of my leg. "Ouch, ouch."

"What is it?"

"Charley horse."

"Which leg?"

"Left one."

He eased his hand down the back of my leg, found the offending muscle, and rubbed it.

The feel of his fingers on my leg blotted out anything else. The charley horse was a minor inconvenience in light of the fact that John was leaning over, his face dangerously near my breasts as his long fingers massaged my leg. I darted a glance to see who was watching. A couple of older women in the stands were staring at me with narrowed eyes and pursed lips. Ladies' League biddies. That had to be it.

"It's good," I said, shamed by their disapproving stares. I was acting unseemly. Not just for a maid, but for any young lady.

"The muscle's still cramping. I can see it twitching."

"John," I said, through gritted teeth. "Stop rubbing my leg, we're being glared at."

He raised his head. "Oh." He straightened. "That's the Baptist minister's wife."

"She looks like she's got a bee in her bonnet."

"Ignore her."

John put an arm on my shoulder and we swayed together to "I'll See You in My Dreams," in no way keeping time to the beat.

We talked during those long hours. About everything under the sun. I told him what it was like to grow up the eldest of seven children with a mother who tended toward poor health. We talked of holidays spent with family, favorite Christmas gifts we'd received. Mine was a cornhusk doll, his a gold-plated kaleidoscope.

John regaled me with stories of his childhood, including the time his father had put him on a horse when he was nine and took him to the top of the Cupid water tower and said, "As far as your eye can see, Johnny, all this land is yours. You're a Fant. People will look to you for direction. When I'm gone, it's all up to you to guide the town to its destiny."

"I can't imagine it."

"I remember being completely overwhelmed," John said.

"You shouldered the responsibility like a prizewinning ox."

He laughed.

"Are you making fun of me?"

"Not at all. I love your idioms."

That word made me feel like a hick. It sounded a whole like "idiot." "What's an idiom?"

"An idiom refers to the way a person phrases things."

"Oh," I said. But that word underscored the differences between us. He was an educated man of the world and I was an apple knocker.

By midnight, my legs felt as if they were set in cement,

heavy hunks that couldn't move. The biddies had left, as had most of the spectators. Twenty couples and twelve hours remained.

At the next break we downed two cups of strong coffee with extra sugar stirred in. The caffeine and sugar jolt carried us through fifteen minutes before we were back to hanging on to each other and swaying to keep each other up.

"Stamina," I murmured at one point.

"What?" John blinked, bleary-eyed.

"You've got lots of stamina."

"So do you."

We grinned at each other and that pepped us up for another few minutes.

By four in the morning, every part of me ached and it felt as if someone had thrust cactus in my eyes. Fresh blood from my blistered toes had oozed through the bandages and dried.

John didn't look much better. His tie was askew and his shirtsleeves were rolled up to the elbow. His hair was mussed, lying every which way. But he looked rakishly handsome with his guard down. I'd seen so many facets of this man—the somber businessman gently breaking bad news, the earthy cowboy who worked the land, the adoring uncle, loyal brother, and now this charming madcap dancer. John Fant was perfect.

My throat clutched. I didn't care about the aches and pains. In fact, they were a badge of honor. I was *glad* I had blisters. John and I were here together. I would never have an opportunity like this again and I was determined to enjoy every miserably wonderful second of it.

All around us, dancers wilted like hydrangeas in the desert. One couple fell asleep on the dance floor, started snoring and stopped moving. A sideline spotter blew a whistle and the couple were out. Forty-two down, thirteen to go.

By five A.M. another couple threw in the towel. Now it was an even dozen. The stands were completely empty, except for one man stretched out sleeping, a fedora cocked over his face.

Only the diligent spotters looked alert.

We were so exhausted. I wasn't thinking straight. I just wanted to stop dancing, but at the same time dreaded the end.

"You can rest your head on me," John invited, and patted his shoulder.

All the other couples were doing it, but John and I weren't really a couple. He was my employer's sister and the owner of the mine where my daddy had been killed. There were some lines that shouldn't be crossed, even in this intimate environment where we'd quickly learned so much about each other.

But his shoulders were so broad and tempting. I glanced around. All the other dancers were engrossed in their own discomfort. No one was watching us except for the two spotters, and the promoter had brought them in so they didn't know us. No clothesline gossip.

Caution flew out the door and I laid my head on his

shoulder, resting my weight against him as I'd done that day on horseback. My knees were trembling and he probably thought it was because my legs were about to give out from all the dancing. He slipped his arm around my waist and whispered, "Steady."

But I wasn't trembling from fatigue.

I made no conscious decision to do so, but my arms slipped around his neck and it seemed as natural as breathing.

"Millie," his lips expelled my name on a soft whoosh of air.

"Mmm," I whispered, my eyelids drooping closed. Sleepy. So sleepy. Sweet dreams.

His thumping heart bounded from his chest into mine and they beat together in one throbbing rhythm that zoomed through my blood, pounded loudly in my ears until I could hear nothing more.

John turned his head. His jaw, barbed with beard stubble, grazed against my cheek. Instinctively, I curled into his soothing warmth and nuzzled my face into the hollow of his neck.

I'm not sure how it happened. Maybe it was me. Maybe it was John. Most likely it was both of us. Our lips were so close and we were clamped together, holding each other and swaying to keep going. Moving my head forward just a quarter of an inch felt so natural.

John's chin lowered.

Our lips brushed.

A bolt of energy shot through me, but instead of pulling away, I pressed closer, wanting more. Oh! Wrong.

Wrong. I know. I know. It seemed so unreal, but at the same time sharper and clearer than anything I had ever experienced.

Suddenly, I was hyperaware of everything.

The band was playing "Why Did I Kiss That Girl?" Irony or inspiration? John's scent mingled with mine, a pleasing musky smell. The texture of his lips, firm but yielding, like the flesh of a ripe plum. The heat between us. The snap, crackle, sizzle.

His mouth captured mine in a kiss so stunning I could not breathe. My head spun, my heart catapulted into my throat. The whole world tilted out of control.

Just as abruptly as he kissed me, John pulled back. "No. We can't do this."

Why? I wanted to beg, but I knew. I wasn't worthy of him.

I blinked away the fog of bliss, looked into his dark chocolate eyes, saw pain and conflict there. He might not want to want me, but he did.

"John," I whispered, not knowing what else to say or do.

He loosened my arms from around his neck, but took my hand. "Millie . . . I have something I should have told you a long time ago, but I thought I could control myself. I never counted on your devastating allure or how this dance marathon would affect us."

I gulped. Hope. Stupidly, I clung to hope. "What is it?"

Anguish carved furrows in his face. "I am betrothed."

Chapter Seven

BETROTHED.

John was engaged to marry another.

But of course. Why was I so shocked? He was twenty-six years old. The head of his family's empire. He required a wife befitting his station and heirs to pass his fortunes down to.

My stomach churned. Why hadn't I known that he was engaged? Why hadn't someone mentioned this woman to me? Mabel loved to gossip sure enough, and yet I hadn't heard a peep about John's betrothal. Why hadn't I ever seen him with this mysterious fiancée? Why was I so dumbly in the dark?

I yanked my gaze from his, stared unseeingly across the dance floor.

"Her name is Elizabeth Nielson," he went on. "We've been betrothed since I returned from the war, but she was too young to get married at the time. Our family advocated the marriage."

"You don't love her?"

"I'm fond of her. You have to understand that a man in my position—"

"I get it," I said. "A man like you could never end up with someone like me."

"I'm so sorry it came to this. I guess I assumed you'd heard about it somehow. Elizabeth has been away at finishing school and then later her aunt fell ill and she stayed in Baltimore to be with her until she recovered. But she's coming home next week. We're getting married on Christmas Eve."

I wanted to tell him to shut up. I didn't care about Elizabeth Nielson. All along I had known that my dreams were folly, but some romantic part of me had spun a fairy-tale world where John and I could somehow carve a future in this bold, brave, more tolerant decade. But it had been nothing but the wild imaginings of a foolish country girl come to town for the first time.

Instinct urged me to flee, to get out of here and take the next train back home, but stubborn pride held me pinned to him, shuffling my battered feet in time to the music. I was not going to let him see how hurt I was. I wouldn't give him that much power over me.

"I didn't expect that you and I would develop feelings for each other," he said. "It was never my intention to mislead you."

I couldn't allow him to keep talking. My stumbling heart could not take it. I threw back my head and laughed.

"Oh, John, I have no earthly idea what you're talking about. I have no feelings for you other than respect."

Yet even I could hear the lie inside my brittle laugh.

"Millie . . ." He looked so utterly wretched that I was almost happy for his pain, but at the same time something inside me tore loose. I loved him too much to want him to suffer.

I closed my eyes. Clenched my jaw. Fought back tears. This was what I got for trying to be something that I was not. "Please," I begged. "Please do not say another word."

He did not.

I could have run away then. Maybe I should have. But if I stayed, if I kept dancing until we were the last couple on the dance floor, I would have a few more precious hours with him before I turned him over to Elizabeth Nielson forever.

Looking sadistically perky, the promoter took the stage and picked up the megaphone.

I groaned aloud. Not again.

"It's time for another Runaround," the promoter announced. "This time, the last six couples will be eliminated."

Half of us. Out.

Part of me longed to throw in the towel, but the part that ached for a few precious hours to hold on to the Cinderella fantasy won out. As soon as the strains of "Rhapsody in Blue" leaked from the clarinet, I tightened my grip on John's hand and we ran as if we were running for our lives.

We made it. Just barely. Me stumbling along in my bloody, tattered bandages, John trying to bolster me without dragging me. We came in sixth out of twelve. Rosalie and Buddy Grass were still in the hunt, but they were bickering. The six eliminated couples looked grateful and staggered for the sidelines.

The rest of us took a short break, then went right back at it.

"Let's not talk anymore," I told John.

He nodded and gathered me into his arms. I rested my head on his shoulder as dawn peeked through the gymnasium windows. Tears slipped down my cheeks and I turned my face into his chest so he could not see, but he felt my grief and tightened his arms around me.

If it hadn't been for the dance marathon I wouldn't have had any of this in the first place, so I took what I could get, and in the midst of the exhaustion, weariness, pain, and suffering, a peaceful calmness settled over me.

I told myself it was enough.

Slowly, the spectators trickled back in. Volunteers brought in fresh food. The smell of bacon, eggs, and coffee made my stomach rumble. By eight A.M. two more couples had dropped out.

Beau brought Penelope back to the gymnasium at ten A.M. During the ten-minute break, we went over to say hello.

"You look like warmed-over death," she declared cheerfully.

"Consider yourself very lucky you sprained your ankle," John said.

"On the upside, you still look better than the rest of the contestants."

Buddy and Rosalie were still bickering. I eavesdropped a bit as I swallowed down a big gulp of hot coffee. It sounded like she was trying to get him to commit to their relationship.

Penelope's eyebrows went up. "My friend Wallis says a dance marathon will either make or break a couple. The sheer endurance and teamwork that it takes to win either makes your bond stronger or shows all the cracks in a relationship. Those two"—she waved at Buddy and Rosalie—"aren't going to make it, and Wallis knows a thing or two about that. She and her husband have separated more times than I can count."

I glanced at John. The marathon had made us closer than ever. Which was precisely the problem; if we hadn't been so close together for so long, these feeling would never have been stirred to this extent.

"Wallis will divorce her husband eventually," Beau predicted. "And she'll be off to make some other poor sap miserable."

"Don't be mean," Penelope said, and tweaked his ear.

He laughed and kissed her affectionately. "I'm just glad you were not a suffragette."

"Wallis wasn't either. She simply has strong ideas about what she wants from life and she's determined to get it. There's nothing wrong with that."

The horn sounded.

"It's back to the dance floor for us," John said, holding me a little less closely now that his family was in the building again.

A few minutes later, another couple dropped out when

the male partner keeled over. Medical personnel rushed in with a stretcher and carted him off.

That left three of us. Me and John, Buddy Grass and Rosalie, and a married couple who had traveled all the way from El Paso to be in the competition. They'd told us during one of the breaks that they were interested in joining the professional dance circuit, and winning the trophy would help get them there. I had no idea there was such a thing as a professional dance circuit.

Time ticked steadily toward noon. Now I knew how Cinderella felt. Soon, the clock would strike twelve. The Nash roadster would turn into a pumpkin. The flapper dress to rags. The sideline spotters and the promoter would turn into mice and scurry off to a field. The glass slipper was already nothing but a bloody bandage.

At fifteen minutes to twelve, the couple from El Paso were disqualified when they stopped moving. It was just us against Buddy and Rosalie, who were still bickering.

"We're going to take this thing," John said.

"I don't know about that. They're feeling frisky enough to fight."

"That might be their ploy to keep going. Stay too mad to fall asleep."

"It's a dangerous strategy."

I gave a halfhearted smile. At this point, I was ready for it all to be over—fall into bed, cry my eyes out, start getting over John. Except I knew there would never be any getting over him. How did you ever get over your one true love?

Twelve noon came and went.

The gymnasium was packed again, people egging us on. It took everything we had in us to keep moving. Every step was painful. Muscles twitched and burned. Gravity pulled on us. Exhaustion sat on our shoulders, whispered lullabies in our ears.

At seven minutes after two o'clock in the afternoon, twenty-six hours after we'd first started dancing, Buddy Grass called Rosalie a rude name.

She slapped his face hard. The loud smack reverberated throughout the entire gym.

The crowd clapped, thrilled by the drama.

Rosalie sank her hands on her hips and proceeded to tell him exactly what she thought of him and his bootlegging ways.

A spotter on the sidelines blew the whistle. "Broken contact. You're out of the competition."

My mind was so foggy, my heart so heavy that it took me a minute to realize that John and I had won the dance marathon. "Give the trophy to your sister," I whispered to him.

"Are you sure you don't want it? You earned it."

I shook my head. The last thing I wanted was a glaring reminder of the romance I'd never had.

People flooded onto the dance floor, separating John and me. They picked us up and carried us on their shoulders to the stage while the band played a rousing version of "It Had to Be You."

Across the heads of the crowd, my eyes met John's, and he looked so sorrowful it ripped my heart out.

We were deposited side by side on the stage in front

of the promoter, who presented us with a trophy and announced that we'd earned the tidy sum of two hundred and fifty-seven dollars for the Ladies' League. It was the most money an event had ever earned for their charity.

"We did it for my sister, Penelope. She deserves all the credit and this trophy," John said, and carried it over to her.

The attention shifted to Penelope, and before anyone noticed me, I turned and slipped away. Nothing to do now but go back to my cramped little room in the maid's quarters and lick my very raw wounds.

JOHN AND I did not speak again after that day. If we saw each other, we'd smile, nod, and then move away from each other as quickly as we could.

"What's wrong with you?" Mabel asked me two days later. "You look as if your favorite cat died."

"Still worn out from all that dancing," I lied.

"I warned you, didn't I?"

"You did."

Penelope was humming happily in the dining room. She'd put the dance marathon trophy on the whatnot shelf and had taken to polishing the brass every day until it shone like gold. The dance marathon was the talk of the town, and even the disapproving old biddies had to admit her methods of raising money—while scandalous—had been quite ingenious. They were already preparing for next year's marathon.

Mabel put a hand to my back. "You're not going to tell me what's wrong?"

I wasn't going to say anything. I promised myself I would never let anyone find out about my foolish infatuation with John, but Mabel smelled too much like home and my tongue just unfurled. "How come you never told me that John was betrothed?"

Mabel looked surprised. "I suppose I sort of forgot about it. He's been betrothed for five years and Miss Elizabeth has been away for most of that time. Is that why you've been mopin'?"

"No," I denied, but I could not meet her eyes.

"I told you that story about Ruthie for a reason."

"I know."

"It didn't stop you from falling in love with him, did it?"

I shook my head, blinked back the tears threatening to slide down my cheeks.

"Ah, wee one." Mabel patted a hand against my back. "He's an easy man to love. So handsome and rich, but kind and thoughtful too. Yours won't be the first heart that broke over John Fant."

"I feel so stupid."

"You can't help who you love." Mabel said sagely. "But you can help acting on it."

I nodded, still unable to speak.

"You'll find a young fellow of your own. One that suits your station."

There it was. The honest truth. Elizabeth Nielson wasn't the real obstacle between John and me—a betrothal could be broken, after all—but rather, our class differences.

I considered leaving my employment and returning to my mother's house, but in the end, I stayed with the Bossiers. I'd changed too much to go back to Whistle Stop. To my mother's mortification, I bobbed my hair, becoming the first woman in Cupid to do so. Cutting my hair was a symbol of liberation. From my past. From my innocence. From John. I'd known heartbreak. It was official. My hairstyle declared me a woman of the world.

I was over John Fant.

Or so I told myself.

By day, I stayed busy, but at night, he would creep into my dreams and I would be a prisoner of my secret desires. Repeatedly, I would awaken bathed in sweat and yearning for something I'd never had.

On the day Elizabeth Nielson arrived home in Cupid, I had taken Addie and Ernest to the park and we were walking past the train station. A glimpse of John stopped me in my tracks, even though both children were tugging on my hands. He was standing on the train platform with his back to me, hand extended to help a beautiful blonde descend from a passenger car.

She was so tiny, probably not much taller than five feet, and petite as a sugarplum fairy. She wore a royal blue dress and had her long, curly hair pulled back with a matching blue ribbon. I put a hand up to my own bobbed curls and for the first time, regretted the cut. She beamed up at John as if he'd hung the moon and sprinkled the sky with stars. Up she went on tiptoes and kissed his cheek. Her lipstick left an imprint of bright red lips on his skin.

He said something to her and she reached up to rub

the lips away with a gloved thumb. Her laugh rang out high and pure, like the sound fine crystal made when tapped with a silver spoon. Of course she would have a perfect laugh. Everything about her was perfect.

I put a hand to the children's backs, anxious to whisk them away before they caught sight of their uncle and wanted to go over and say hello. "Hurry on, children. We must get you home to wash up before dinner."

But I couldn't resist glancing over my shoulder for one last look.

Instantly, I regretted it.

Because John was staring at me over the top of his fiancée's head. Our eyes met, sparked like two flint stones off each other, and it was a sorrowful second. He looked as miserable as I felt.

Immediately, we both turned away. Me to the children. Him to Elizabeth.

My pulse throbbed at my throat and my mouth flooded with a briny taste. It was only then that I realized I'd swallowed my tears. What else could I do?

Love was one thing.

Reality, quite another.

Chapter Eight

I DID MY BEST to reconcile the fact that John was getting married on Christmas Eve. I stayed busy, worked hard cleaning and decorating, helping Mabel with the cooking and watching the children. I went home to see my family on the fourth Sunday of every month, and while I enjoyed visiting there, it seemed each time I was moving further and further from my roots.

I felt detached, adrift, caught between two worlds. I wasn't really part of the Fant family, but I no longer fit in with my own family either. I'd changed too much. I'd danced and worn short skirts and cut my hair and . . . and . . . kissed a man who was engaged to another.

Shamed, I kept to myself as much as possible.

Wedding plans were in high gear now that Elizabeth was back in town. There were fittings for Penelope and Addie's dresses to wear to the wedding and new shoes ordered from the Montgomery Ward catalog. Elizabeth came to call on occasion, asking Penelope's opinion on this or that.

She was a vapid girl who prattled on and on and on about nothing and everything, but I harbored no ill will toward her. She'd had her claim on John long before I'd come to Cupid. I was the interloper, not she. My poor luck to have fallen for a man I could not have.

The butcher's son asked me out and I agreed to go. We shared an ice cream sundae at the drugstore soda fountain. He talked of the various cuts of meat as I stared out the plate glass window, watching people go by.

John and Elizabeth came into view. He had her little hand tucked in his big one. My heart careened in my chest and I heaved in a deep sigh.

With uncanny timing, John turned his head and stared right at me. Kissed my face with his eyes. We both startled at the unexpected whap of silent contact. He jerked his attention back to Elizabeth at the same time I cupped my chin in my palms and said to my date, "Tell me more about the New York strip."

By the week before Christmas, I stopped pretending not to care about John's upcoming nuptials. I couldn't eat. Mabel noticed my weight loss. She pinched my ribs, clicked her tongue, said, "Pining ain't gonna help nothing, eat sumpthin'."

Penelope said I could have Christmas Eve and Christmas Day off to visit my family, and that was a relief, not to be in Cupid on John's wedding day, but when I wrote my mother to tell her this, she said she and the kids were going on the train to visit my aunt Sweenie in San Antonio for Christmas. She invited me to come, but I couldn't be gone the length of time it would take to get to San Antonio on the train and back.

So I was stuck.

"You'll come to the wedding with us," Penelope said cheerfully. "You can't spend Christmas Eve all alone."

"It's not my place, ma'am," I said. "I'm just the help."

She pondered that a moment. "Do whatever makes you comfortable, Millie, but you're welcome to sit with my family."

After she left the kitchen, Mabel shook her head. "That woman can be dense sometimes. No wonder Ruthie got in a family way right underneath her nose." Then she invited me to come spend Christmas with her and her oldest daughter in Marfa, but I turned Mabel down too.

All right. I will admit it. Two days before Christmas Eve I was feeling pretty sorry for myself. I had decorated someone else's tree. Baked Christmas cookies with someone else's children. Watched someone else prepare to marry the man I loved madly.

I lay in bed that night, buried under thick wool blankets, staring up at the ceiling, recalling what had led me to be here. Losing my daddy. Tears rolled down my cheeks. I felt so utterly alone.

How could John marry Elizabeth when he was simply fond of her? She could never love him the way I did.

Cupid! What cruelty to have flung his arrows at John and me when we could never be.

I lay there cursing Cupid, but then I remembered the story Rosalie had told me in the Cupid Caverns about

Mingus Dill and Louisa Hendricks. How in despair Mingus had gotten down on his knees and prayed before the stalagmite and his life had been spared by Louisa's love.

Praying to a stalagmite seemed a bit too blasphemous for me, but what if instead of a prayer, I wrote Cupid a letter? Might that work just as well?

Besides, what did I have to lose?

Inspired, I leaped from the bed and went to the small writing desk in the corner of my little room. I lit a candle, pulled out a piece of paper and the inkwell from the desk and sat down to write.

Dear Cupid,

How heartless of you to make me fall in love with a man who is out of my reach.

My love for John Fant took me unaware. It was not planned nor anticipated nor even wanted, but once it was upon me, I can think of nothing else but him.

He is my beloved, my one and only, my one true love, and yet I can never breathe the word of this to anyone. It is my sorrow that he belongs to another, and even if he didn't, the chasm between us is so wide. Him on one side, me on the other.

We pass each other in the street, our eyes meet, and the longing is so big you can punch it, but we must not touch, must not say what's on our minds. Quick, we look away, scurry off, unfulfilled and aching.

So hard. We hide our love. Not only from prying

eyes, but from each other. I want to shout my love for him to the world. Stand atop the Davis Mountains and shout it down into the valley for everyone to know. I cannot. I dream sweet dreams of the hot fires of perfect love and wake to cold embers.

Such a misery. Such a curse. This love that can never be.

Oh, Cupid! Don't be cruel. Break his bond with the other woman. Build a bridge we can cross. Bring him to me. Let my dreams be fulfilled or let me fall forever asleep, and awaken only when his lips touch mine.

I beseech you with all my heart. Help him find a way to me or release me from this desperate burning love.

Forever Hopelessly in Love

My tears dropped on the paper, smeared the ink. I folded the letter, slipped it in an envelope. I had no plan in my head. Driven by pain, sorrow, love, and longing, I tucked the letter into one pocket of my thin wool winter coat, a flashlight in the other. In the dead of night I crept from the servants' quarters. The half moon lighted my path through the silent streets of Cupid. My breath chuffed out in frosty puffs, but I felt no cold. I was on a mission.

The walk was long and steep. I toiled up the mountain to the Cupid Caverns, my fingers curled around the letter in my pocket. I felt as desperate as Mingus Dill must have felt the night the sheriff's posse cornered him in the cave. But I was at my wits' end. I had nowhere else to turn.

Coyotes yipped in the distance. Creatures rustled in the bushes. I might have been afraid if I hadn't been raised in the country, knew the night sounds like an astronomer knew the stars. I trudged and daydreamed. Thought about the marathon. "It Had to Be You" circled around and around in my head. Finally, I reached the caverns.

The night road might not have scared me, but stepping into that cavern took extra courage. Only thoughts of John kept me going. This was my last-ditch effort. Useless, most likely, but it was all I had. Something was better than nothing.

Please, Cupid, please.

A fresh cold blasted my face as I stepped into the cavern. My hands shook as I shone the thin flashlight beam around, found the wandering path, and started my journey.

At one point I thought I was lost and a breath-stealing panic grabbed my lungs as I realized no one knew where I was. If I took a wrong turn and found myself wandering endlessly, no one would know to come look for me.

I contemplated going back, but then there I was, in the cave with the Cupid stalagmite looming over me. I crouched beside it. Imagined Mingus Dill in this spot pleading for his life.

Love had saved Mingus. Maybe it could save me too.

I left the letter at Cupid's feet, left my beating heart and endless hopes and shattered dreams there too.

Have it all, Cupid. It was all or nothing. John or a lifetime of unfulfilled yearning.

I stumbled from the cave, made my way through the cavern, and popped out into the moonlight. I remembered the last time I'd left the caverns and walked this road. John had come upon me and given me a ride.

I touched my cheek. The one that I had rested against his back.

"John, I love you!" I yelled the words out loud. It felt so good that I said it again. And again. Spilling to the heavens the words I could never ever say to him.

"I love you, John. Marry Elizabeth if you must, but it will never change how I feel. I'll love you until my dying day."

The wind whistled through the mesquite trees and a light sprinkling of snow started to fall. My toes were cold. Nothing to do now but let go.

My fate was in Cupid's hands.

I SPENT CHRISTMAS Eve morning in my room. I did not want to get in the way of the family's wedding day preparations. Nothing had happened since I left the letter at Cupid's feet. I don't know what I expected. A bolt of lightning from the sky? John's life path had been set long before I ever met him. It was unreasonable to expect him to change it for me.

Hope is a terrible thing. It keeps you clinging when you should let go. It sails you straight onto rocky shoals.

Nothing is going to happen, Millie, I told myself. *Go back to sleep. When you wake, John and Elizabeth will be married and all hope will be gone.*

But sleep was impossible.

I got up, got dressed, and with hands clasped behind my back, I paced the small room. The wedding was at eleven, with a reception brunch to follow at the Fants' home. All I had to do was peek out the window and I'd be able to see the guests arriving with presents when the time came.

I couldn't do it. I couldn't stay here and watch.

Out. Get out of here. I wrestled into my coat and put on mittens my mother had knitted me for Christmas. She'd sent them in the post on the same day she told me that she and my brothers and sisters were going to San Antonio.

For the longest time, I simply wandered around town. Everywhere I went people smiled and wished me Merry Christmas. I forced a smile, wished them the same, but inside I was hollow as a Halloween jack-o'-lantern.

I swear I had no intention of stepping into the First Methodist Church of Cupid. Why torture myself by watching John hitch himself to Elizabeth for life? But as more and more people, decked out in their Sunday best finery, streamed past me headed for the church, I found myself helplessly following the crowd.

Don't do it, Millie. Don't.

I stopped on the sidewalk outside the limestone church with a tall silver steeple reaching for the sky. Had the silver come from the Fant mine? Could my daddy have mined it? Were there other silver steeples stretching across the Southwest? A trail of my father's work. A legacy linking past to future for generations to come. The notion pleased me.

A relentless wind whipped down off the mountains, stirred the skirt of my work dress around my legs. I wasn't dressed for church services, much less a Christmas Eve wedding.

The crowd was thinning as eleven o'clock approached, and still I stood rooted. Paralyzed by indecision.

I pictured myself running up the aisle and just as the preacher asked if anyone knew a reason these two should not be joined to speak now or forever hold their piece, yell out, *I know a reason. John loves me and I love him.*

Of course I would not, could not do that, no matter how much my heart was breaking. If there was to be a miracle, John would have to come to me. I would not throw myself at him.

An image of my letter, lying at Cupid's feet, drifted into my mind. I'd have to go back up there and retrieve the letter before someone else found it and learned of my lovesick secret.

But not today. I was too weary. Maybe tomorrow as everyone else celebrated Christmas.

The bell clock in the tower of the Catholic church across the street chimed the hour. Eleven o'clock. Elizabeth would be walking down the aisle.

I curled my hands into fists, waited. The sidewalk around me was empty. The final stragglers had already entered the church. I should leave. Go back to my room.

My feet ignored my brain. Before I knew it, I had

climbed the steps and my sweaty palm was on the doorknob. Strains of the bridal march drifted through the heavy wooden door.

"No. No. Don't do it," I whispered.

Was I talking to myself? Or John?

I twisted the knob, eased open the door. Lighted candles flickered. The ends of the pews were decorated with red poinsettias and white bows. The scent of pinecones filled the air. A wizened old lady pounded the keys of the organ, pumping out the slow-paced song. Elizabeth, looking like a china doll, was being escorted down the aisle on her father's arm. Every seat was taken and numerous guests stood along the back wall. Rosalie and Buddy Grass were among those standing. Apparently, they had gotten back together. It seemed most everyone in town had come out to see Cupid's heir apparent take his bride.

There was no room for me here.

Go.

Common sense finally sank in and I was just about to turn away when I spied John standing at the end of the aisle, dressed in a dapper black suit, his hands clasped in front of him. My stomach flopped over and I forgot to breathe.

His eyes met mine.

I saw in them anguish that mirrored my own. I wanted to flee, but my feet were rooted to the spot. I knew one thing with absolute certainty. If I moved, my knees would collapse, so I stood in the doorway, hung in darkness as black as the Cupid Caverns at midnight. Why, oh why had I opened that door?

Elizabeth and her father reached the altar.

But John was not looking at his bride. He only had eyes for me.

My lips parted and I whispered inaudibly, "My one true love."

Elizabeth's father turned her over to John, stepped back, and seated himself in the front pew. John took Elizabeth's hand.

Torture. This was pure torture I had to go. Somehow I would force myself out the door. On jelly legs, I turned.

The preacher cleared his throat, but before he could speak, John cried, "Wait."

I stopped, imagining he was speaking to me, but I did not dare turn back in case he was not.

The entire church went utterly silent.

"Elizabeth," John said, his voice strong and clear. "I cannot marry you. While you are a wonderful person and I regret causing you pain, I truly love another."

The congregation let out a collective gasp.

Slowly, I pivoted back to face the front of the church. My heart was pounding so hard I wondered if others could see it beating against my chest.

Elizabeth paled, swayed on her feet, let out a quiet little peep.

"I'm sorry," John told her. "But it's better to say it now than enter into a marriage where neither of us would be happy."

Elizabeth's eyes were wide as plates. "Who . . . who is this woman you love?"

John stretched out a hand to me. "I love Millie Greenwood."

The second collective gasp was louder than the first.

In hindsight, I probably should have slipped out the door and let him come find me once the commotion was over, but I simply could not contain myself. I flew down the aisle toward his outstretched arms.

He grabbed me in his arms, spun me around, dropped a hundred kisses on my face in between whispering, "I love you, I love you, I love you."

"I love you too," I said, tears streaming down my cheeks, and for a moment I feared it was all a sweet dream.

"No!" a loud female voice called out from the back of the room. "No! This isn't right."

John and I broke apart.

Quickly, I cast a glance at Elizabeth, who seemed rather numb. She blinked repeatedly. Her parents went to her side and were patting her hand, but she shook them off. "I'm fine. John's right. He doesn't love me and I don't love him. We were just merging our money and family names."

I swung my gaze to the congregation, stared into a sea of faces, all with various shades of reaction. Some looked shocked. Some smiled knowingly. Some scowled. One older woman muttered, "This is what comes of women having the right to vote. Utter chaos."

But the woman who'd shouted was now waving a white envelope in her hand and marching toward the altar. I recognized both the woman and the envelope.

It was Rosalie Smithe and she had my letter.

"*She* doesn't get to be Cinderella. She doesn't get to marry the prince. This is all wrong. She's a *maid.*"

"What's wrong with that?" someone called out, and I realized it was Beau Bossier. "Rich or poor. You love who you love."

"But that's just it." Rosalie marched up to me, shook the letter underneath my nose. "John doesn't really love you, does he, Millie?" She spun back to face the congregation. "This maid has bewitched John Fant and I have the proof."

There was more gasping and rustling of skirts. A cold chill shoved straight down my spine.

Rosalie opened the envelope, unfolded my letter, and began to read it. "Dear Cupid, How heartless of you to make me fall in love with a man who is out of my reach."

When she finished reading, she added, "Millie Greenwood bewitched him. She wrote a letter to a heathen god asking him to cast a spell on Mr. Fant."

My knees turned to water. All the air left my body. I couldn't look at John for fear I'd see betrayal on his face.

Rosalie's face turned red.

"How do we know Millie wrote that?" Penelope asked. "It's signed, Forever Hopelessly in Love."

"It's her handwriting." Rosalie passed the letter to Penelope.

Penelope read the letter with an impassive face and passed it to her mother.

"Where did you get the letter?" the preacher asked from behind us.

I startled. Held my breath.

"My boyfriend, Buddy Grass, saw her coming out of the caverns at midnight, night before last. He found it at the base of the Cupid stalagmite."

"What was Buddy doing up there in the caverns in the middle of the night?" The town sheriff stood up and cast a glance down the aisle at Buddy, who was easing out the back door.

The congregation was muttering about spells and witches and Cupid and blasphemy and all manner of dark things.

"Really," Elizabeth said. "It's all right. I think it's all for the best."

I was liking her more and more and feeling guilty for the pain I was causing her, but what worried me was how John was taking the reading of my letter to Cupid. I raised my head and met his eyes, terrified to see condemnation there.

But his eyes were soft and kind. "Hush!" he commanded the room. "I have something to say."

Everyone fell silent. The runaway groom had spoken.

John faced me, took my hand, held it tightly in his. "It's true. Millie Greenwood has bewitched me."

That drew more comments, murmurs, and gasps from the crowds.

"But not in the way Rosalie suggests. Millie has bewitched me with not only her beauty, but her kindness, her good nature, and her willingness to help others. She bewitched me with her smart mind and sensible outlook. It does not matter to me that she is a maid. Or that she wrote a letter to Cupid begging for intervention. It only proves how she much loved me if she was desperate enough to write a letter and walk it all the way up to the Cupid stalagmite in the middle of the night."

"Yes," I whispered because it was true.

"You're the one that I love, Millie Greenwood. For better or worse and everything in between."

"Oh, John!" I whispered, too happy to cry.

He gathered me up into his arms and with everyone watching carried me out of the church as if I were his bride.

Epilogue

I MARRIED JOHN FANT eighteen months later on the best day of my life. Not in a church with a silver fancy steeple—we were known for bucking convention, after all—but in front of the silver mine where my daddy had died. I saw it as a fitting tribute to my father. A new beginning where a tragic ending had taken place. The mine would reopen the following day after John's painstaking restoration. He'd taken it beyond the safety standards of even the most secure mineshaft in the country.

Something unexpected had happened in the renovations. They found a new vein of ore no one knew about, and so his kind caring and attention to detail paid off.

My mother moved my sisters and brothers to San Antonio to live near her sister, and while I hated not having them nearby, it was time for my family to begin a new chapter of their lives, just as I was.

And John's family? They welcomed me into the family

with open arms. Ultimately, they just wanted their son to be happy, and it was as clear as the smiles on our faces that we made each other happy.

What happened that day in the First Methodist Church became known all throughout the Trans-Pecos region, and a funny thing happened. People began marking pilgrimages to the Cupid stalagmite and leaving letters asking for his help in affairs of the heart. Side business sprang up to take advantage of this unexpected tourist trade. Inns were built and local business started selling Cupid merchandise. It was a heady time. Times were changing. All the old rules were breaking and people were becoming more accepting of new ideas and new ways of doing things.

By writing that letter to Cupid, I'd started something bigger than myself.

And as John and I sealed our marriage with a heartfelt kiss, a legend was born.

GO WILDE THIS SUMMER!
Here is a sneak peek at

LOVE AT FIRST SIGHT

Available May 28, 2013

and

ALL OUT OF LOVE

Available June 25, 2013

The first two books in *New York Times* bestselling author Lori Wilde's delicious new series set in Cupid, Texas!

Love at First Sight

Just one look and the earth
trembled beneath my feet.
—Millie Greenwood

Dear Cupid,

The most awesomely awful thing has happened. I have fallen truly, madly, deeply in love.

Awesome because I have never felt anything like this. I've heard people talk about love at first sight, but I never believed in it. Then with just one look—bam! I was a goner. The minute we laid eyes on each other we knew we were destined soul mates. Suddenly, our minds are wide open and the world is the most beautiful place. How have I gone so long without knowing magic like this?

But that's what you do, isn't it, Cupid? Fling your

arrow and make people fall in love at first sight. Drive them crazy. Send them over the edge of reason.

It's awful because I've been accepted into Oxford University with a full scholarship. I can't bear the thought of leaving my guy behind, and family responsibilities keep him from joining me in England. My head tells me that this is a once-in-a-lifetime opportunity and I can't pass it up, but I ache at the thought of being so far away from him. What's the point of the finest education in the world if you can't be with the one you love? Tell me what to do, Cupid. Go or stay? My fate is in your hands.

—Shot Through the Heart

Natalie McCleary folded the well-creased letter and tucked it into the pocket of her Van Gogh yellow sundress. The letter writer's angst settled in the pit of her stomach. Sometimes, playing Cupid was more difficult than running her bed-and-breakfast, Cupid's Rest.

It had been over a week since the letter had arrived and she still had no answer for the sender. Her response had the power to change the entire trajectory of Shot Through the Heart's future, and she did not take her duties lightly.

The trouble was, at twenty-nine, Natalie herself had never been in love. Who was she to give advice to the lovelorn?

You're Millie Greenwood's direct descendant, that's who. It's your obligation whether you want it or not.

Wasn't that just the story of her life? Obligation. Responsibility. Tradition.

Natalie shook her head and squared her shoulders. *C'mon, don't be resentful.* She'd never been a complainer or shirker and she wasn't about to start now.

The sole of her right yellow Keds made a slight scraping sound as she scuffed over terra-cotta paver stones. She moved toward the large white wooden box situated underneath the cherubic fountain in the botanical gardens, located in the center of downtown Cupid, Texas. It was just after dawn and the gardens weren't yet open to the public, but in another two hours the place would overflow with tourists.

Mockingbirds called from pink-blossomed desert willows. Over by a prickly pear cactus, a black-crested titmouse gobbled up a fat grub worm. Undisturbed by Natalie's presence, a long-legged roadrunner strolled over the limestone rock wall surrounding the gardens. Locusts started a low-hummed buzzing, tuning up for the encroaching late June heat. Dragonflies hovered over the fountain, and a toad peeked up at her from blue pebble gravel around the firecracker plants. From La Hacienda Grill down the street, the smell of huevos rancheros wafted on the air and mingled with the perfume of fuchsia rockroses.

The morning seemed to be holding its breath, waiting for something to happen. For what, she didn't know, but the notion dug in so deeply that she hesitated, caught her breath, and glanced around.

Nope, no one, she was totally alone.

You're losing it, woman.

She cocked her head, listening, but heard nothing

out of the ordinary. Off in the distance an eighteen-wheeler ground its gears as it churned up the mountain. The rhythmic sound of a garbage truck's backup beeper drifted over from First Street, followed by the mechanized wheeze of the lifting arm and the clattering clang of a Dumpster being emptied. From the stables behind the gardens, a horse whinnied.

Home.

Still the same, but oddly different somehow.

Inexplicably, goose bumps spread over her skin. She rubbed her arms with her palms.

Weird.

Junie Mae Prufrock, who owned the LaDeDa Day Spa and Hair Salon next door to Natalie's B&B, would claim that someone had walked over her grave.

Shrugging off the unwanted sensation, Natalie twirled the combination lock on the white wooden box marked "Letters to Cupid" in stenciled red block print. The lock popped open and she raised the lid.

As usual, it was stuffed with letters. She pinched up the full skirt of her shirtwaist dress with one hand, forming a sling to hold the letters as she emptied the box. The dewy morning air kissed her knees. After one-handing the padlock closed, she limped over to the bicycle she'd left parked on the pathway and deposited the letters into the wicker basket strapped to the front.

One swoop of her foot released the kickstand. She slung her leg over the cruiser saddle seat and she was off, pedaling through the back of the garden to the dirt-packed alley that ran between the gardens and the stables.

The wind ruffled her hair, brought with it the scent of horses. A long-tailed flycatcher perched on a telephone line, its split tail hanging underneath it like scissors. She smiled as the sun warmed her face, more at ease on a bike than she ever was on her feet. When she rode, no one could see her limp.

She bumped through the alley, turned left on Murkle Street, and waved to Deputy Calvin Greenwood, who was also a cousin. Calvin was coming out of the Divine Bakery with two boxes of doughnuts in his arms and headed for his patrol car.

Smiling, she waved a hand, paused in the middle of the road.

"Morning, Nat," he called. "Lots of love letters this week?"

"Usual Monday morning. Cupid's got his hands full."

"That's a good thing, right? Keeps our economy rolling." Cal balanced the doughnut boxes in one hand while he opened his cruiser door with the other.

"You can say that again."

"Maybe you should write a letter yourself."

"To Cupid?"

"Yeah."

"Why would I do that?"

"So you'd have a date to mine and Maria's wedding next month."

Natalie snorted good-naturedly. "Cal, there's no such thing as Cupid."

"Shh." He pressed an index finger to his lips. "Don't let that get out. Maria thinks that's how she caught me."

"Any sign of Red?" Natalie asked him about her long-term boarder who'd disappeared four days ago without a word of warning. It wasn't the first time Red had gone missing, so she was trying not to worry too much, but he'd left all his possessions behind.

"Haven't seen him, but you know these war vets." Calvin shrugged. "They ain't like regular folks. Red can take care of himself."

"But you're still keeping an eye out for him?"

"'Course."

"Now you're just patting me on the head."

"He's a drifter at heart, Natty. I warned you about that when he moved in."

"That's the issue. He doesn't have anyone else to worry about him."

"Your heart's too big, cousin. It can't hold the whole world."

"Doesn't have to hold the whole world. Just my corner of it."

"Funny that he disappeared the day the rent was due."

"If he just left, why didn't he take his things?"

"Tell you what, I'll do some more asking around," Calvin promised. "Now I gotta get to work. Have a good day."

"Don't eat too many doughnuts," she hollered over her shoulder as she took off again, the bike picking up speed on the downhill slope.

She had so much to do that morning—take the letters to the community center for Aunt Carol Ann to sort out, cut fresh flowers for the guest rooms, make sure Zoey got up in time to make it to her anatomy class at Sul Ross, greet the guests at breakfast, order organic multigrain flour before her cook, Pearl, actually followed through on her idle threats to quit, and make a decision about Red. She didn't want to give his room away, but if he wasn't coming back, she needed to rent it out.

Natalie had put off the decisions because she kept thinking that Red would pop back up as he usually did, but something felt different this time. Lately, he'd become more reclusive than usual and he'd taken to wearing a John Deere ball cap and dark sunglasses ninety percent of the time, as if he was trying to vanish behind the thin disguise. Maybe he had just walked away, leaving her on the fence about what to do.

After she finished all those morning tasks, she had to head back to the community center for lunch and the tri-weekly meeting of the Cupid committee volunteers, where they gathered to answer the letters written to Cupid. This Monday she wasn't looking forward to the meeting. The other women were bound to ask why she hadn't already answered Shot Through the Heart's letter.

Why? Because she couldn't think of a single word of useful advice.

Her hand strayed again to the letter in her pocket. She fingered the edges, mentally toying with her reply. She wanted so badly to tell the letter writer that there was really such a thing as love at first sight, but Natalie was having her own crisis of faith.

It was the central conflict she wrestled with every time she answered a love letter. Dishing out advice when she had no clue what she was talking about. She'd expressed her self-doubts to the group, but they'd waved away her concerns.

"Listen to your heart," they always said. "You know the truth, deep down inside."

Yeah? Well, her heart was telling her she had no business responding to the letters considering that she'd never been in love. She'd wanted to be in love, had imagined it happening to her a thousand times. How could she not, in a town chockful of romantic legends?

She'd dated six men in her entire life, had kissed four of them but slept with none. She'd been holding out for that one special man.

Except he'd never come.

Waiting had been easy enough when she was younger. She'd been starry-eyed and hopeful. Her limp had made her shy and self-conscious, but she was convinced that the right man would see through all that if she only held out for him.

Then the years rolled away.

She'd gotten swept up in running the B&B and riding herd on her sister, Zoey, but she'd kept the faith. But then as the years kept clicking by, she'd started having doubts. What if it was all bunk? What if there wasn't one right man for her? What if she'd missed out on some genuinely nice guys simply because she didn't give them a chance because she'd never felt the magic?

Now, on the precipice of turning thirty, her virginity was an albatross. An embarrassment. How did you bring that up in conversation on a date? *Would you like to be the one to deflower me? Take me for my maiden voyage? Pop my cherry?*

But this was the part that really bothered her.

What if she just got on with her life, gave up her shaky belief in love at first sight and all that other romantic stuff, found a decent guy, married him, and then The One finally came along?

Then again, what if The One never showed up? Was she expected to live her entire life without sex, without a husband, without kids while she waited around on a fantasy?

She was of two minds. Her heart desperately wanted to believe, but at her core, she was a pragmatist.

"Just you wait," Aunt Carol Ann would say. "When it hits, you'll know. There will be absolutely no doubt."

Natalie wished she could get her faith back, but the last few years her aunt's promise sounded as much of a fairy tale as Cupid with his bow and arrow, flying around shooting people through the heart.

"You're too practical for your own good, Natty," Junie Mae told her at least once a month. Usually when they sat on Junie Mae's front porch sipping sweet iced tea spiked with lemon and eating sugar cookies. "You need to brush up against Zoey, see if some of her spontaneity will rub off on you."

That hurt.

Natalie didn't particularly enjoy being the sensible sister, but someone had to be the responsible one and since she was the older, she'd been elected by default. Sure, she'd love to be like Zoey, twenty-two and still working on finishing her college degree because she'd flakily changed her major four times. Her sister had dabbled in—and ditched—criminal justice, natural resource management, and musical theater. Now she was hung up on the idea of being an archeologist.

Solid career plan, sis.

Her bike clipped along at twenty-five miles an hour, kept pace with her racing mind, until she slowed to round the corner onto Main, and suddenly there he was, big and unexpected.

A naked man.

No, not naked, her brain corrected, catching up to what her eyes saw, just gloriously shirtless.

Speechless, she stopped pedaling.

He was in the empty Piggly Wiggly parking lot, head down, bending over a big black motorcycle as he tinkered with the engine. His torso was leanly muscled, darkly tanned, and glistening with sweat in the early morning sunlight.

The hair on his head was the color of a raven's wing, so black it looked almost blue, and curled unkempt around his ears and down the nape of his neck. His powerful biceps flexed as he worked. A sexy dark blue tattoo graced his left upper arm. His abdominal muscles were taut as drum skins. A pair of black jeans hung low on his hips, and he wore well-used cowboy boots.

His masculinity was palpable and she could have sworn she caught a faint whiff of his scent, aftershave and motor oil and something sensually seductive—danger.

But that was foolishness. Danger didn't have a smell, and besides, she was yards away.

His cheekbones, cast in shadows, looked sharp as blades. His chin was pure granite and peppered with stubble. Natalie's practicality vanished as wild fantasy took her hostage with tumbling images—leather tool belts, muscle cars, Desert Eagle pistols, campfires, and mountain lions.

Honest to Pete, she didn't know men could look like that outside of movie reels. Her jaw dropped, and all the breath left her lungs. She stared, stunned.

Natalie saw him in a freeze-frame flash of blind clarity. A click-whirl snapshot caught in time. Her mouth went instantly dry and her heart slam-pumped blood through her ears. Oh my. Oh dear. Oh no. He's here.

He reached for a red rag to wipe his hands, straightening to his full height. He stood well over six feet tall, sturdily built and breath-stealingly impressive.

The moment hung in the air, tremulous as a spiderweb spun under eaves in a rainstorm, but bright, sharp, clear, and unmistakably special.

As Natalie coasted past, their gazes locked.

In that fraction of a blink, she memorized everything about him. Eyes the color of coal, chiseled jaw, Olympic shoulders, hard everywhere, all of him bottled into an explosive package.

Boom!

His eyes pierced into her like an arrow's point, took her, owned her.

Dear God! What was this?

A lazy, wolfish, one-sided grin spread slowly across his face.

Just one look and all the mysteries of the universe were answered. Every nerve ending in her body tingled to life as if she'd been asleep for a hundred years and was awakening for the very first time.

It's him!

He was a stranger to Cupid. She did not know him, had never met him, and yet, in that hushed sweet second, her body knew something that her mind did not. She felt him deep in her center.

At last.

He'd found her at last.

It struck her like a fever, hot and rushed, an emotion so sudden and sweet that her brain fumbled and stupidly came up with the word "love."

Did she dare think it? How foolish to think such a thing of a stranger. No. Not love. Love at first sight was absurd, right?

And yet . . . and yet . . .

Panic spread through her as more images fell in on her. His big, black cowboy boots parked underneath her bed, her sunny yellow Keds lined up beside them. Warm quilts on a cold winter night. Silver lightning that lingered—burning and brilliant. His hard mouth crushed against her soft one, tasting rich and decadent as pure dark chocolate.

What did it all mean?

She had no explanation for what she was feeling. It

was too blissful. Too good. It scared the living crap out of her.

Thankfully, gratefully, she'd already sped past him. She was too terrified to glance back.

A mirage, she told herself. A dream. Not real. He could not be real.

The blood had drained from her face, leaving her cheeks quite cold. Ghostly. The road flattened, her pace slowed. She tried to get her legs moving again, but they were cement, too heavy to move.

Craziness.

This was sheer craziness. She'd lived in Cupid too long and even though she didn't believe in the love legends, apparently the stories had been like the creeping damp, silently, insidiously closing in on her to culminate in this . . . this . . . What the hell was *this*?

She swallowed, listening to the quickening of her pulse, felt the blood rush fierily back to her cheeks, and suddenly, she could not see. Oh, everything was still there—the trees, the buildings, and the vehicles—but the image imprinted on her retina was not of the scenery before her. Instead, his face blotted out everything else, like a full solar eclipse turning high noon to midnight.

Music filled her vision—violins and saxophones, pianos and drums, Vivaldi and Mozart, Pachelbel and frickin' Bonnie Tyler. Colors surrounded him—a rainbow of pleasure—crimson, azure, olive, lavender, saffron.

Could she be having a stroke?

Yes. A stroke. That might explain the wild euphoria, the ceaseless pounding of her heart, the inability to breathe. Why couldn't she breathe?

"When it hits, you'll know." Aunt Carol Ann's words rang in her head. "There will be absolutely no doubt."

Dear Cupid, the most awesomely awful thing has happened.

DAZZLED, DADE VEGA blinked and she was gone.

He shook his head, wondering if he'd imagined the phantom beauty in yellow on the pale blue Schwinn, looking like springtime in Paris. Why did it feel as if the bottom had just dropped out of his world?

A hard tightening gripped him in all the right places. He scrubbed a sheepish palm over his face. Purposefully, he stepped to the curb and glanced down the street.

Nothing. Nobody.

She was gone, if she'd ever really been there at all.

It wouldn't be the first time he'd had a hallucination, but it would be the first time since the head injury he'd suffered in Afghanistan four years ago.

Ah shit. Man, he couldn't backslide, not after all the progress he'd made. If he was backsliding, it's had everything to do with Red's disappearance.

Funny how easy it was for the past to reach up and punch you in the face when you least expected it.

Honestly, he was half hoping that she *was* a hallucination because that would rightly explain the berserk push-pull between his head and his heart. He felt a rushing need to go after her, spill his guts, tell her who he was and how he felt. One look in her enigmatic sky blue eyes and he felt as if love beckoned him with open arms, while his soul had dug in its heels and jerked back, too guilty of damage and sin to believe anything so good could be true.

He knew better.

Life had kicked Dade in the teeth far too many times for him to trust it. He'd learned that happiness, by and large, was a mirage and it was best not romanticized.

But the woman's image lingered, leaving an indelible imprint, and he found himself thinking about a soft mattress on a hot sweaty night, sheets tangled up in their entwined limbs. He could almost hear her calling out his name in ecstasy, and dammit if he didn't start to get hard.

False, this vision, he knew it, but he could still see her delicate lightness, her smile, modest and a little shy, but as welcoming as warm socks on a cold winter's day. A tumble of soft brown hair floating out behind her like a cloud as she rode past.

For that instant when she'd looked at him and he'd looked at her, one lonely soul connecting with another, Dade had thought, *It's her.*

It was a stupid thing to think, he was well aware of that, but he'd thought it nonetheless.

Forget it. Move on.

Moving on was the only way he'd survived, another lesson courtesy of the Navy SEALs. It was harder to hit a moving target. Red had proven the point. His friend had stopped in Cupid, stayed, gotten comfortable, and now he'd gone missing after texting Dade a Mayday message three days earlier.

Tanked.

The secret code only they understood. It meant *I'm in trouble deep, trust no one.*

That's why he was here in this dead-end, desert mountain town. To find out what had happened to his foster brother who'd also served with him in the SEALs. They'd joined the navy together the day after they graduated from high school, and Red was the only person in the whole world that Dade gave a shit about. Because of that, he'd taken a leave of absence from the security detail he'd been on in New Orleans.

There were no commercial flights into Cupid and since the nearest big airport was in El Paso, two hundred miles away, he decided to simply make the drive. Waiting around in airports made him feel helpless. At least when he was on the road, he was making progress. Unfortunately, he'd been out on an oil derrick in the Gulf of Mexico when the text had come through, and it had taken him this long to arrive.

He was terrified that Red had gone off his meds and was in the grips of full-blown, post-traumatic stress flashbacks. After the Mayday message, Red had not answered any of Dade's calls or texts. Tough as he was on the outside, his buddy was as emotionally fragile as an eight-year-old.

Dade had to be careful. He couldn't afford to assume it was simply PTSD. What if Red had stumbled across something or found himself in some other kind of trouble? He was here to retrace his buddy's steps. The best way to do that was to ease himself into the community and see what he could find out.

First his junkie parents, and then the foster care system, had taught him that trusting people was a damn dumb thing to do, so his plan was to keep his connection to Red a secret until he got the lay of the land and figured out where his buddy had gone.

Which was another reason he was particularly disturbed by his overwhelming reaction to the woman on the bicycle. It simply wasn't smart.

There she was again, clogging up his mind—that pretty oval face, big blue eyes, and full pink lips. He imagined she smelled like honeysuckle. When he and Red were kids, they used to pluck the white blooms from the honeysuckle vines that grew up the wooden privacy fence of their foster home, break them open, and suck out the drop of sweet nectar.

Kissing her would be like that.

Honeysuckle woman, that's how he thought of her now.

For Chrissakes, Vega, knock it off. If she's even real, she's way out of your reach for so many more reasons than you can count.

He might as well wish for the Hope Diamond. He was as equally likely to possess it. Dade pulled a palm down his face, winced at the prickle. He hadn't shaved since the previous day and he haired up fast thanks to his father's Hispanic blood, Satan rest the bastard's soul.

"Screw it," he muttered, and wrestled into the T-shirt he'd stripped off while working on his motorcycle.

The trip through the desert and up the Davis Mountains had messed with the Harley's timing and he'd had to disassemble the gas tank to get to the timing belt. The job had taken over an hour and he'd been putting the chopper back together when she'd ridden past.

He'd stopped underneath the security lamps in the Piggly Wiggly parking lot because it had still been dark when he'd started the job. Dade packed up his tools, stuffed them in the compartment underneath the seat, and wondered what honeysuckle woman's name was.

Forget her already.

He strapped on his helmet, slung his leg over the machine, reached down to turn on the check valve. Instantly, fuel poured from the tank, soaking the leg of his pants in gasoline.

Dammit!

In his stunned enchantment with the woman on the bicycle, he'd neglected to reattach the hose.

All Out of Love

Millie Greenwood High School,
Cupid, Texas, May 25, 2001

Dear Cupid,

I am crazy in love with my older brother's best friend, Pierce Hollister! You should see him in his gym shorts when he's out on the football field running sprints. Omigod, he's got the most amazing thighs. Of course that's nothing compared to the way his butt looks in Wranglers. Be still my pounding heart!

And his eyes! Brown with intriguing green flecks.

He made direct eye contact with me once. It was a moment I will never, ever forget until my dying day. I'd dropped my books in the crowded hallway and I was fumbling to pick them up when suddenly, out of nowhere, I see a pair of black cowboy boots and a hand reaching out to help me.

I looked up and it was him!

I got tingly all over and honest to God, I thought I was going to die right there on the spot! This is no ordinary boy. He's the quarterback of the football team! He dates cheerleaders! His daddy owns the biggest ranch in Jeff Davis County and here he was helping me!

And I'm nobody. I'm pudgy (Mama calls me fluffy) and I wear glasses and I stutter. I've had speech therapy, but I still can't speak without stammering and that is in a relaxed atmosphere. Believe me there was nothing relaxed about this. Every muscle in my body was tuned as tight as the strings on a concert violin and I couldn't have said a word if my life depended on it.

His eyes met mine and he smiled.

Smiled! At me!

"Here you go," he said, handing me my biology book (it had to be biology, didn't it?), and our knuckles brushed. I don't know how I kept from bursting into flames. "Have a nice day, Lace."

And then he was gone, leaving his heavenly sunshine and leather scent lingering behind, as I stared after him with my mouth gaping open.

Pierce Hollister had smiled and touched my hand and said eight whole words. To me!

I have no chance with him. I know that. He's a senior. I'm a freshman. He's handsome as a movie star. Way out of my league. He's filet mignon and I'm day-old bread. Okay, so I am a direct descendant of Millie Greenwood, but so are practically half the people in this town. It's not a unique claim to fame.

It's silly of me to wish and pine, I know. But Cupid, I just can't stop thinking about him, no matter how much I try. Every night before I go to sleep, I imagine what it would feel like if he were holding me tight against his muscled chest, our hearts beating in perfect time together. Beating as if we were one.

That's why I'm writing to you, Cupid. I'm miserable with love for him. I want him to love me back so badly that I can barely breathe. Please, Cupid, please let Pierce Hollister fall in love with me. I know I'll have to wait for him. I am only fourteen after all and he's got a girlfriend and a football scholarship to the University of Texas, but one day? Someday? Please!

Yours in total despair,
Hopelessly Tongue-Tied

Lace Bettingfield stood frozen in freshman homeroom, half in the doorway, half out of it, with her backpack slung over one shoulder.

Seated in front of her were seventeen students, and every single one of them was reading the current issue of the school newspaper, the *Cupid Chronicle*.

Ominously, hairs on the nape of her neck stood up.

The fact that *everyone* was reading—including the stoners and the jocks—was odd enough, but when they all looked up at her with what seemed to be perfectly choreographed smirks, Lace's stomach took the express elevator to her Skechers.

In a split second, her gaze darted to the student nearest her. It was Toby Mercer, her biology lab partner.

Toby was six-foot-six and weighed the same as Lace, a hundred and sixty-two pounds; on him the weight was gaunt, on her it was zaftig. He possessed strawberry blond hair and skin so pale it had earned him the nickname Casper way back in kindergarten. She'd known him her entire life. His family lived just down the block from hers. She'd comforted him when kids had picked on him. They'd attended each other's birthday parties. They'd dissected frogs together.

But right now, Toby was looking at her all narrow-eyed and smug, like she was a dilapidated barn and he was a wrecking ball.

She flicked her eyes from Toby's face to the paper he held in his hand, and there it was.

Dear Cupid,

I am crazy in love with Pierce Hollister!

It was the letter she'd written to Cupid, her private letter that had never been meant for anyone's eyes but her own, printed on the front page of the school newspaper!

Her letter. Front page. Declaring her love for Pierce.

How? How had this happened?

Unlike the tourists who came to Cupid, wrote letters

to the Roman god of love, and deposited their letters in the special letter box in the botanical gardens (expecting them to be answered by the town's volunteers and published in the weekly Cupid Chamber of Commerce circular), Lace had never intended for anyone to see this letter.

She'd written it in study hall three days earlier as she gazed out the window, watching the football team practice. She'd carefully folded the letter and tucked it into the side pocket of her notebook with every intention of burning it in the patio chiminea that weekend when her parents were out of town at a cutting horse event.

Reality hit her like a fist to the face.

Mary Alice.

Mary Alice Fant, her second cousin, who was also the editor of the *Cupid Chronicle*. Pierce had recently dumped her for the head cheerleader, Jenny Angus. Two nights ago, Mary Alice and her parents had come over to Lace's house for dinner, and at one point, Lace had caught Mary Alice snooping around in her bedroom.

Oh God!

Now everyone knew about her secret crush. Her life was ruined. Nausea splashed scalding bile into her throat. Her entire body flushed hot as August in the Chihuahuan Desert.

One heartbeat later, and the class erupted into a feeding frenzy.

"Do you imagine she calls out Pierce's name when she's touching herself?" sniggered Booth Randal, a smart-assed stoner who spent the bulk of his time in detention.

"P . . . Pa . . . Pa . . . Pa . . . Pierce," another boy stuttered in a fake falsetto, "Yo . . . yo . . . yo . . . you . . . ma . . . ma . . . make me so hot."

Moaning and breathing heavily, the two boys pretended to kiss and fondle each other, while the other students hurled derisive catcalls like stones.

"Poor me," wailed Tasha Stuart, whose mother worked in the teller cage next to Lace's mom at Cupid National Bank. "I'm sooo in love with the most popular boy in school and he doesn't know I exist."

"Who knows," someone else called out. "She might stand a chance. Pierce could be a closet chubby chaser."

"Na . . . na . . . na . . . not unless she can sta . . . sta . . . stop stutt . . . stutt . . . stuttering." Toby stabbed her in the back.

"Yeah, who wants a girl whose tongue is hopelessly tied?"

"One day. Someday."

"Please, Cupid, please, please, please."

The words slapped her harder than any physical blow. She knew these people. Was related to some of them. Had thought many of them were her friends, but they'd turned on her like hyenas.

The only one who looked at her with anything other than ridicule was Pierce's younger brother, Malcolm. He slunk down in his seat, pulled his collar up, sank his chin to his chest, and kept his eyes trained on his hands folded atop his desk. He was embarrassed for her humiliation.

Blindly, Lace spun on her heels, and almost crashed into the teacher, Mr. Namon.

He put up his palms, "Whoa, slow down, what's going on, Miss Bettingfield?"

Head ducked, Lace shoved past him and fled down the corridor.

But there was no sanctuary here.

The hallways were lined with students, several of them holding copies of the *Cupid Chronicle*. Some laughed. Some pointed. Some made lewd gestures. Some threw out more catcalls. A goth girl was slyly singing "Crush," a song about a stalker.

Everyone was going to think she was a stalker.

"Hey, Tongue-Tied, drop thirty pounds and maybe you can land your dream man."

"Reality check. No guy like Pierce could ever love someone like you."

"Yes, he touched your hand, but I heard he washed it off in Lysol afterward."

Lace plastered her hands over her ears, willed herself not to cry, but it was too late, tears were already streaming hotly down her cheeks.

Nightmare. It was a living nightmare.

And just as in a nightmare everything moved in slow motion. It felt as if she was trying to run through knee-deep mud. Her lungs squeezed tight. Her heart pounded so hard she thought it was going to beat right out of her chest.

Good. If her heart beat out of her chest she would die.

It seemed to take hours to traverse that hallway. She kept her head down, didn't once make eye contact with anyone. She was headed for the exit, desperate to find a place to lick her wounds.

The morning sun glinted against the metal bar in the middle of the exit door. Almost there. Salvation was just a few steps away. She rushed forward, her legs breaking through the slow-motion morass.

Her hand hit the bar and she gave a hard shove.

But fate, that vicious bitch, wasn't done with her yet.

The door smacked into something solid. Someone was coming in at the same time she was trying to get out. Trapped. She was trapped. No exit. *Knock 'em down if you have to. Just get the hell out of here.*

She raised her head and found herself staring into Pierce Hollister's brown eyes.

Her heart literally stopped and a whimper escaped her lips.

For Mary Alice to print her letter in the school paper was a horrible betrayal. The bullying by classmates she thought she knew was unbearable. Breaking down and crying in front of everyone was humiliating, but nothing that had happened to her that morning was as bad as what was written across Pierce's handsome face.

Utter, abject pity.

About the Author

LORI WILDE is the *New York Times* bestselling author of more than forty-five books. A former RITA® finalist, Lori has received the *Romantic Times* Reviewers' Choice Award, the Holt Medallion, the Booksellers Best, the National Readers' Choice, and numerous other honors. Lori teaches Romance Writing Secrets via the Internet through colleges and universities worldwide at www.ed2g.com. She lives in Weatherford, Texas, with her husband and a wide assortment of pets.

Contact Lori via her home page at www.loriwilde.com.

Visit www.AuthorTracker.com for exclusive information on your favorite HarperCollins authors.

About the Author

Lori Wilde is the *New York Times* bestselling author of more than forty-five books. A former RITA finalist, Lori has received the Romantic Times Reviewers' Choice Award, the Holt Medallion, the Bookseller's Best, the National Readers' Choice, and numerous other honors. Lori teaches Romance Writing Seminars via the internet through colleges and universities worldwide at www.ed2go.com. She lives in Weatherford, Texas, with her husband and a wide assortment of pets.

Contact Lori via her home page at www.loriwilde.com.

Visit www.AuthorTracker.com for exclusive information on your favorite HarperCollins authors.

Give in to your impulses . . .
Read on for a sneak peek at five brand-new
e-book original tales of romance
from Avon Books.
Available now wherever e-books are sold.

STEALING HOME

A Diamonds and Dugouts Novel

By Jennifer Seasons

LUCKY LIKE US

Book Two: The Hunted Series

By Jennifer Ryan

STUCK ON YOU

By Cheryl Harper

THE RIGHT BRIDE

Book Three: The Hunted Series

By Jennifer Ryan

LACHLAN'S BRIDE

Highland Lairds Trilogy

By Kathleen Harrington

An Excerpt from

STEALING HOME

A Diamonds and Dugouts Novel

by Jennifer Seasons

When Lorelei Littleton steals Mark Cutter's good luck charm, all the pro ball player can think is how good she looked . . . and how bad she'll pay. Thrust into a contest of wills, they'll both discover that while revenge may be a dish best served cold, when it comes to passion, the hotter the better!

Raising his glass, Mark smiled and said, "To the rodeo. May you ride your bronc well."

Color tinged Lorelei's cheeks as they tapped their glasses. But her eyes remained on his while he took a long pull of smooth aged whiskey.

Then she spoke, her voice low. "I'll make your head spin, cowboy. That I promise."

That surprised a laugh out of him, even as heat began to pool heavy in his groin. "I'll drink to that." And he did. He lifted the glass and drained it, suddenly anxious to get on to the next stage. A drop of liquid shimmered on her full bottom lip, and it beckoned him. Reaching an arm out, Mark pulled her close and leaned down. With his eyes on hers, he slowly licked the drop off, his tongue teasing her pouty mouth until she released a soft moan.

Arousal coursed through him at the provocative sound.

Pulling her more fully against him, Mark deepened the kiss. Her lush little body fit perfectly against him, and her lips melted under the heat of his. He slid a hand up her back and fisted the dark, thick mass of her long hair. He loved the feel of the cool, silky strands against his skin.

He wanted more.

Tugging gently, Mark encouraged her mouth to open for him. When it did, his tongue slid inside and tasted, explored the exotic flavor of her. Hunger spiked inside him, and he took the kiss deeper. Hotter. She whimpered into his mouth and dug her fingers into his hair, pulled. Her body began pushing against his, restless and searching.

Mark felt like he'd been tossed into an incinerator when he pushed a thigh between her long, shapely legs and discovered the heat there. He groaned and rubbed his thigh against her, feeling her tremble in response.

Suddenly she broke the kiss and pushed out of his arms. Her breathing was ragged, her lips red and swollen from his kiss. Confusion and desire mixed like a heady concoction in his blood, but before he could say anything, she turned and began walking toward the hallway to his bedroom.

At the entrance she stopped and beckoned to him. "Come and get me, catcher."

So she wanted to play, did she? Hell yeah. Games were his life.

Mark toed off his shoes as he yanked his sweater over his head and tossed it on the floor. He began working the button of his fly and strode after her. He was a little unsteady on his feet, but he didn't care. He just wanted to catch her. When he entered his room, he found her by the bed. She'd turned on the bedside lamp, and the light illuminated every gorgeous inch of her curvaceous body.

He started toward her, but she shook her head. "I want you to sit on the bed."

Mark walked to her anyway and gave her a deep, hungry kiss before he sat on the edge of the bed. He wondered what she had in store for him and felt his gut tighten in anticipation. "Are you going to put on a show for me?" *God, it'd be so hot if she did.*

All she said was "mmm hmm." Then she turned her back to him. Mark let his eyes wander over her body and decided her tight, round ass in denim was just about the sexiest thing he'd ever seen.

When his gaze rose back up, he found her smiling over her shoulder at him. "Are you ready for the ride of your life, cowboy?"

Hell yes he was. "Bring it, baby. Show me what you've got."

Her smile grew sultry with unspoken promise as she reached for the hem of her t-shirt. She pulled it up leisurely while she kept eye contact with him. All he could hear was the soft sound of fabric rustling, but it fueled him—this seductively slow striptease she was giving him.

He wanted to see more of her. "Turn around."

As she turned, she continued to pull her shirt up until she was facing him with the yellow cotton dangling loosely from her fingertips. A black, lacy bra barely covered the most voluptuous, gorgeous pair of breasts he'd ever laid eyes on. He couldn't stop staring.

"Do you like what you see?"

Good God, yes. The woman was a goddess. He nodded, a

little harder than he meant to because he almost fell forward. He was starting to tell her how sexy she was when suddenly a full-blown wave of dizziness hit him. He shook his head to clear it. *What the hell?*

"Is everything all right, Mark?"

The room started spinning, and he tried to stand but couldn't. It felt like the world had been tipped sideways and his body was sliding onto the floor. He tried to stand again but fell backward onto the bed instead. He stared up at her as he tried to right himself and couldn't.

Fonda stood there like a siren, dark hair tousled around her head, breasts barely contained—guilt plastered across her stunning face.

Before he fell unconscious on the bed, he knew. Knew it with gut certainty. He tried to tell her, but his mouth wouldn't move. Son of a bitch.

Fonda Peters had drugged him.

An Excerpt from

LUCKY LIKE US

Book Two: The Hunted Series

by Jennifer Ryan

The second installment in The Hunted Series by Jennifer Ryan . . .

1

A wisp of smoke rose from the barrel of his gun. The smell of gunpowder filled the air. Face raised to the night sky, eyes closed, he sucked in a deep breath and let it out slowly, enjoying the moment. Adrenaline coursed through his veins with a thrill that left a tingle in his skin. His heart pounded, and he felt more alive than he remembered feeling ever in his normal life.

Slowly, he lowered his head to the bloody body lying sprawled on the dirty pavement at his feet. The Silver Fox strikes again. The smile spread across his face. He loved the nickname the press had given him after the police spoke of the elusive killer who'd caused at least eight deaths—who knew how many more? He did. He remembered every one of them in minute detail.

He kicked the dead guy in the ribs. Sonofabitch almost ruined everything, but you didn't get to be in his position by leaving the details in a partnership to chance. They'd had a deal, but the idiot had gotten greedy, making him sloppy. He'd set up a meeting for tonight with a new hit but hadn't done the proper background investigation. His death was a direct result of his stupidity.

"You set me up with a cop!" he yelled at the corpse.

He dragged the body by the foot into the steel container, heedless of the man's face scraping across the rough road. He dropped the guy's leg. The loud thud echoed through the cavernous interior. He locked the door and walked through the deserted shipyard, indifferent.

Maybe he'd let his fury get the best of him, but anything, or anyone, who threatened to expose him or end his most enjoyable hobby needed to be eliminated. He had too much to lose, and he never lost.

Only one more loose end to tie up.

2

San Francisco
Thursday, 9:11 p.m.

Little devils stomped up Sam's spine, telling him trouble was on the way. He rolled his shoulders to erase the eerie feeling, but it didn't work, never did. He sensed something was wrong, and he'd learned to trust his instincts. They'd saved his hide more than once.

Sam and his FBI partner, Special Agent Tyler Reed, sat

in their dark car watching the entrance to Ray's Rock House. Every time someone opened the front door, the blare of music poured out into the otherwise quiet street. Sam's contact hadn't arrived yet, but that was what happened when you relied on the less reputable members of society.

"I've got a weird vibe about this," Sam said, breaking the silence. "Watch the front and alley entrances after I go in."

Tyler never took his eyes off the door and the people coming and going. "I've got your back, but I still think we need more agents on this. What's with you lately? Ever since your brother got married and had a family, you've been on edge, taking one dangerous case after another."

Sam remembered the way his brother looked at his wife and the jealousy that had bubbled up in his gut, taking him by surprise. Jenna was everything to Jack, and since they were identical twins, it was easy for Sam to put himself in Jack's shoes. All he had to do was look at Jack, Jenna, and their two boys to see what it would be like if he found someone to share his life.

Sam had helped Jenna get rid of her abusive ex-husband, who'd kidnapped her a couple years before. Until Jack had come into her life, she'd been alone, hiding from her ex—simply existing, she'd said. Very much like him.

An Excerpt from

STUCK ON YOU

by Cheryl Harper

Love's in the limelight when big-shot producer KT Masters accidentally picks a fight with Laura Charles, a single mother working as a showgirl waitress in a hotel bar. When he offers her the fling of a lifetime, Laura's willing to play along . . . just so long as her heart stays out of it. If she can help it, that is!

Laura said, "Excuse me, Mr. Masters." When he held up an impatient hand, she narrowed her eyes and turned back to the two women. "Maybe you can tell him the drinks are here? I've got other customers to take care of."

The pink-haired woman held out a hand. "Sure thing. I'm Mandy, the makeup artist. This is Shane. She'll do hair. We'll both help with costumes and props as needed."

As Laura shook their hands, she privately thought that might be the best arrangement. Shane's hair was perfect, not one strand out of place. Mandy's pink shag sort of made it look like she'd been caught in a windstorm. In a convertible. But her makeup and clothes were very cute.

KT said, "Hold on just a sec, Bob. Let me go ahead and tweet this. Gotta keep the fans interested, you know."

Laura glanced over her bare shoulder to see KT bound down the stairs, pause, snap a picture, and then type something on his phone before shouting about taking down the electronic display in the corner. Lucky would not be happy about that. As KT waved his arms dramatically and the director nodded, Laura smiled at the two girls. "Guess I'm dismissed."

They laughed, and Laura turned to skirt their table as she reached for the drink tray. Being unable to move, like her feathers had attached themselves to the floor, was her first clue that something had gone horribly wrong. And when KT Masters bumped into her, sending the tray skidding into the sodas she'd just delivered, she knew exactly who was responsible. She tried to whirl around to give him a piece of her mind but spun in place and then heard a loud rip just before she bumped into the table and sent two glasses crashing to the floor. She might have followed them, but KT wrapped a hand around her arm to steady her. His warm skin was a brand against her chilly flesh.

The only sound in Viva Las Vegas was the tinny *plink* of electricity through one million bright white bulbs. Every eye was focused on the drama taking place at the foot of the stage. Before she could really get a firm grip on the embarrassment, irritation, shock, and downright anger boiling over, Laura shouted, "You ripped off my feather!"

Even the light bulbs seemed to hold their breath at that point.

KT's hand slid down her arm, raising goose bumps as it went, before he slammed both hands on his hips, and Laura shivered. The heat from that one hand made her wonder what it would be like to be pressed up against him. Instead of the flannel robe, she should put a KT Masters on her birthday list. She wouldn't have to worry about being cold ever again.

"Yeah, I did you a favor. This costume has real potential"—he motioned with one hand as he looked her over from collarbone to knee—"but the feathers get in the way, so . . . you're welcome!" The frown looked all wrong on his face, like he didn't have a lot of experience with anger or irritation, but the look in his eyes was as warm as his hand had been. When he rubbed his palms together, she thought maybe she wasn't the only one to be surprised by the heat.

They both looked down at the bedraggled pink feather, now swimming in ice cubes and spilled soda under his left shoe. No matter how much she hated the feathers or how valid his point about their ridiculousness was, she wasn't going to let him get away with this. He should apologize. Any decent person would.

"What are you going to do about it?" She plopped her hands on her own hips, thrust her chin out, and met his angry stare.

He straightened and flashed a grim smile before leaning down to scrape the feather up off the floor. He pinched the driest edge and held it out from his body. "Never heard 'the customer's always right,' have you?"

Laura snatched the feather away. "In what way are you a customer? I only see a too-important big shot who can't apologize."

His opened his mouth to say . . . something, then changed his mind and pointed a finger in her face instead. "Oh, really? I bet if I went to have a little talk with the manager or Miss

Willodean, they'd have a completely different take on what just happened here and who needs to apologize."

Laura narrowed her eyes and tilted her head. "Oh, really? I'll take that bet."

An Excerpt from

THE RIGHT BRIDE

Book Three: The Hunted Series

by Jennifer Ryan

The Hunted Series continues with this third installment by Jennifer Ryan . . .

1

Shelly swiped the lip gloss wand across her lips, rolled them in and out to smooth out the color, and grinned at herself in the mirror, satisfied with the results. She pushed up her boobs, exposing just enough flesh to draw a man's attention, and keep it, but still not look too obvious.

"Perfect. He'll love it."

Ah, Cameron Shaw. Rich and powerful, sexy as hell, and kind in a way that made it easy to get what she wanted. Exactly the kind of husband she'd always dreamed about marrying.

Shelly had grown up in a nice middle class family. Ordinary. She desperately wanted to be anything but ordinary.

She'd grown up a plump youngster and a fat teenager. At fifteen, she'd resorted to binging and purging and starved herself thin. Skinny and beautiful—boys took notice. You can get a guy to do just about anything when you offer them hot sex. By the time she graduated high school, she'd transformed herself into the most popular girl in the place.

For Shelly, destined to live a glamorous life in a big house with servants and fancy cars and clothes, meeting Cameron in the restaurant had been a coup.

Executives and wealthy businessmen frequented the upscale restaurant. She'd gone fishing and landed her perfect catch. Now, she needed to hold on and reel in a marriage proposal.

2

Night fell outside Cameron's thirty-sixth-floor office window. Tired, he'd spent all day in meetings. For the president of Merrick International, long hours were the norm and sleepless nights were a frequent occurrence.

The sky darkened and beckoned the stars to come to life. If he were out on the water, and away from the glow of the city lights, he'd see them better, twinkling in all their brilliant glory.

He couldn't remember the last time he'd taken out the sailboat. He'd promised Emma he'd take her fishing. Every time he planned to go, something came up at work. More and more often, he put her off in favor of some deal or problem that couldn't wait. He needed to realign his priorities. His daughter deserved better.

He stared at the picture of his golden girl. Emma was five now and the image of her mother: long, wavy golden hair and deep blue eyes. She always looked at him with such love. He remembered Caroline looking at him the same way.

They'd been so happy when they discovered Caroline was pregnant. In the beginning, things had been so sweet. They'd lain awake at night talking about whether it would be a boy or a girl, what they'd name their child, and what they thought he or she would grow up to be.

He never thought he'd watch his daughter grow up without Caroline beside him.

The pregnancy took a turn in the sixth month when Caroline began having contractions. They gave her medication to stop them and put her on bed rest for the rest of the pregnancy.

One night he'd come home to find her pale and hurting. He rushed her to the hospital. Her blood pressure spiked, and the contractions started again. No amount of medication could stop them. Two hours later, when the contractions were really bad, the doctor came in to tell him Caroline's body was failing. Her liver and kidneys were shutting down.

Caroline was a wreck. He still heard her pleading for him to save the baby. She delivered their daughter six weeks early, then suffered a massive stroke and died without ever holding her child.

Cameron picked up the photograph and traced his daughter's face, the past haunting his thoughts. He'd spent three weeks in the Neonatal Intensive Care Unit, grieving for his wife and begging his daughter to live. Week four had been a turning point. He felt she'd spent three weeks mourning the loss of her mother and then decided to live for her father. She began eating on her own and gained weight quickly. Ten days later, Cameron finally took his daughter home. From then on, it had been the two of them.

Almost a year ago, he'd decided enough was enough. Emma needed a mother.

An Excerpt from

LACHLAN'S BRIDE

Highland Lairds Trilogy

by Kathleen Harrington

Lady Francine Walsingham can't believe Lachlan MacRath, laird and pirate, is to be her escort into Scotland. But trust him she must, for Francine has no choice but to act as his lover to keep her enemies at bay. When Lachlan first sees Francine, the English beauty stirs his blood like no woman has ever before. And now that they must play the besotted couple so he can protect her, Lachlan is determined to use all his seductive prowess to properly woo her into his bed.

May 1496
The Cheviot Hills
The Border Between England and Scotland

Stretched flat on the blood-soaked ground, Lachlan MacRath gazed up at the cloudless morning sky and listened to the exhausted moans of the wounded.

The dead and the dying lay scattered across the lush spring grass. Overhead, the faint rays of dawn broke above the hilltops as the buttercups and bluebells dipped and swayed in the soft breeze. The gruesome corpses were sprawled amidst the wildflowers, their vacant eyes staring upward to the heavens, the stumps of their severed arms and legs still oozing blood and gore. Dented helmets, broken swords, axes, and pikes gave mute testimony to the ferocity of the combatants. Here and there, a loyal destrier, trained to war, grazed calmly alongside its fallen master.

Following close upon daylight, the scavengers would come

creeping, ready to strip the bodies of anything worth a shilling: armor, dirks, boots, belts. If they were Scotsmen, he'd be in luck. If not, he'd soon be dead. There wasn't a blessed thing he could do but wait. He was pinned beneath his dead horse, and all efforts to free himself during the night had proven fruitless.

In the fierce battle of the evening before, the warriors on horseback had left behind all who'd fallen. Galloping across the open, rolling countryside, Scots and English had fought savagely, until it was too dark to tell friend from foe. There was no way of knowing the outcome of the battle, for victory had been determined miles away.

Hell, it was Lachlan's own damn fault. He'd come on the foray into England with King James for a lark. After delivering four new cannons to the castle at Roxburgh, along with the Flemish master gunners to fire them, he'd decided not to return to his ship immediately as planned. The uneventful crossing on the *Sea Hawk* from the Low Countries to Edinburgh, followed by the tedious journey to the fortress, with the big guns pulled by teams of oxen, had left him eager for a bit of adventure.

When he'd learned that the king was leading a small force into Northumberland to retrieve cattle raided by Sassenach outlaws, the temptation to join them had been too great to resist. There was nothing like a hand-to-hand skirmish with his ancient foe to get a man's blood pumping through his veins.

But Lord Dacre, Warden of the Marches, had surprised the Scots with a much larger, well-armed force of his own, and what should have been a carefree rout had turned into deadly combat.

A plea for help interrupted Lachlan's brooding thoughts.

Not far away, a wounded English soldier who'd cried out in pain during the night raised himself up on one elbow.

"Lychester! Over here, sir! It's Will Jeffries!"

Lachlan watched from beneath slit lids as another Sassenach came into view. Attired in the splendid armor of the nobility, the newcomer rode a large, caparisoned black horse. He'd clearly come looking for someone, for he held the reins of a smaller chestnut, its saddle empty and waiting.

"Here I am, Marquess," the young man named Jeffries called weakly. He lifted one hand in a trembling wave as the Marquess of Lychester drew near to his countryman. Dismounting, he approached the wounded soldier.

"Thank God," Jeffries said with a hoarse groan. "I've taken a sword blade in my thigh. The cut's been oozing steadily. I was afraid I wouldn't make it through the night."

Lychester didn't say a word. He came to stand behind the injured man, knelt down on one knee, and raised his fallen comrade to a seated position. Grabbing a hank of the man's yellow hair, the marquess jerked the fair head back and deftly slashed the exposed throat from ear to ear. Then he calmly wiped his blade on the youth's doublet, lifted him up in his arms, and threw the body facedown over the chestnut's back.

The English nobleman glanced around, checking, no doubt, to see if there'd been a witness to the coldblooded execution. Lachlan held his breath and remained motionless, his lids still lowered over his eyes. Apparently satisfied, the marquess mounted, grabbed the reins of the second horse, and rode away.

Lachlan slowly exhaled.

Sonofabitch.